OPERATION LARGE SCOTCH

by

Bill Flockhart

Edinburgh :: 2017

Chapter 1

Looking out at the rain lashing down on the Antrim
University campus, Michael Caldwell announced to the
assembled body, 'May 25 1998 was a sad day for our
movement when the entire population of the Emerald
Isle fell for Tony Blair's publicity machinery and voted to
end the struggle which those of us in this room have
been waging for the last thirty years. Maybe Gerry
Adams and Martin McGuiness have decided the fight is

over and they have won their place in history but I'm sure I speak for us all when I say the fight must go on.'

Michael was referring to the Good Friday Agreement when the majority of people throughout the whole of Ireland agreed to a future of co-operation between the governments of the North and South of the country. There was opposition to the move from the Democratic Unionist party but international support for the initiative meant that it gained acceptance.

'Aye, I agree with you Michael it's been at a great cost - too many young lives have been ended prematurely by British bullets, interjected Seamus Carr, before continuing to puff on his slim panatela.

Michael continued, "So how does this change our future? Well for a start, fund-raising will be affected if and when the public decide that they no longer have to succumb to our cause as the population have voted 71% in Northern Ireland and amazingly 94% in the South to support the peace initiative. The Garda on both sides of the border will be co-operating much more closely and using MI5 intelligence data to flush us out. On a personal front the disruption campaign has provided us, the High Command, and to a lesser extent our foot soldiers, with a far higher standard of living than we otherwise would have experienced in our lifetime. We have been able to skim off money from the protection rackets and drug trafficking. The proceeds have been laundered safely out of Northern Ireland into tax havens around the world. Why, there's nobody in this room who doesn't have a seven figure bank balance tucked away in a foreign bank for their old age."

The other five in the room nodded.

"Well it was good while it lasted" muttered Pat Kearney, a white-haired veteran of the terrorist movement, "I'll just have to send the wife out to work!" he laughed.

David Cossar was not amused, adjusting his hornrimmed spectacles he solemnly addressed his colleagues "I do not take defeat lightly - especially from the likes of Tony Blair who once this agreement is finalised will probably come clean and join the Catholic Church - making him almost one of us. I said years ago that we should stick to our principles and not get distracted into filling our own pockets, but use all the funds to support our communities. Now as a result of yesterday our intelligence network will be fractured as there will not be the same level of confidential information circulating amongst ourselves. That will make our communities attractive to organised crime movements, who have always left us alone in the past as they feared reprisals emanating from our network of look-outs. This looks like the end for us Michael."

Michael Caldwell, the Chancellor of Antrim University, looked down at his colleagues around the table before replying "Well only if we allow it to be, and I for one have no intention of letting other organisations profit at our expense. We have to keep a lid on our income sources but change our opus memorandum on how we go about our business. There will be no more city centre mass killings using car bombs as this will only result in adverse publicity, bringing the security services and the official IRA down on us. I began giving this matter some thought for some time now as the opinion polls began to prophesy the result of the Peace Initiative and I think we

4

should concentrate on hurting the British Government where it matters - in their pocket."

Colm Murphy, the Party Treasurer, stirred, "Do you have anything specifically in mind Michael?" He enquired.

"Yes" Michael confirmed "but it is not for discussion today. Meeting over"

The 1972 Club, as they chose to call themselves in memory of Bloody Sunday, rose from their seats, making small talk about their families and how their local football team was performing. Michael indicated that he would join them shortly in 'The Sands Bar' as it was known to republicans once he had finished tidying up. As they sauntered out it gave him time to analyse his command team.

Pat Kearney had been raised in Londonderry, "It's Derry, mention London and I'll knock your bloody head off!" He warned all and sundry. He had been present on Bloody Sunday, when British troops opened fire on republican demonstrators killing 13 demonstrators, including seven children. That led to him joining the IRA. Although not a military man but one with a strong physical presence, he quickly adapted to the training he received and soon demonstrated a talent for carrying out the 'awkward jobs' - placing bombs under the cars of the unsuspecting and carrying out assassinations. His reputation soon spread and 'PK' became feared in the republican communities. It was soon recognised the control he displayed in these areas was invaluable. The younger members in the movement were brought up by their parents to respect 'PK', who was now in his late fifties, as the last thing they wanted was him to come knocking on their door.

The financial guru Colm Murphy was the antithesis of PK. A first in economics at Queen's University was followed by Colm graduating as a Chartered Accountant whist working at PWC who sent him across the water to 'the Golden Mile' to get experience in the workings of the investment market. The young accountant took to it like a duck to water and quickly learned to move large sums of money around the world to such an extent that he became a recognised authority on the subject. This did not go unnoticed by Michael Caldwell who invited Colm to consider a career in academia. Knowing full well that being a good Catholic boy raised in the Bogside he would be missing home and was ideal to administer the considerable cash-flow collected by the republican hierarchy from their faithful supporters. A family man, married with three children living in leafy Dunmurray, he was highly regarded in the community - even among the Protestant professionals and academics.

Seamus Carr was the 'motivator' of the movement using his training skills to keep all the members faithful to the cause at all times - even if this meant handing out punishments including tarred & feathering which still existed for those who took the British pound in return for information. Children are the lifeblood of any protest movement and Seamus took a pride in organising, in conjunction with the local priesthood, youth clubs where he would observe the kids, looking for future recruits the Provisionals required to keep the Cause alive. Seamus a single man had a dark side that attracted him to young boys which he disguised under the cover of his interest in the youth centres.

Michael Caldwell's reign had modernised the republican movement in Londonderry but in order to implement the programme he needed the services of a top IT guru and he found the perfect answer in Mhairi McClure. At 40 she was younger than the other council members and from a completely different if somewhat privileged background. Not one for campaigning in the street demonstrations, preferring instead to be seen at the Irish horse racing meetings in both Northern Ireland and Eire. An attractive rather than beautiful woman with Nordic blond hair, piercing green eyes and a slim figure, Mhairi could scheme with the best of them and gather intelligence through her social contacts. Mhairi had, after an all-girls public-school education obtained a place at Oxford where she gained a first in computer studies before doing a Master's degree at Harvard. Boston opened Mhairi's eyes (and her legs) to the opposite sex and to the charms of Matt O'Reilly in particular, a descendant of a prominent Bay Stater Irish family who had left the 'old country' during the potato famine and had prospered into one of the richest dynasties in Boston.

After suffering a personal tragedy Mhairi applied and successfully obtained a lecturer's position at Antrim University where she met Michael Caldwell who nurtured her attributes and put them to good use for his political agenda. Her fiancé Matt O'Reilly's sudden death had greatly affected Mhairi's long-term plans to marry into the O'Reilly family and, rather than take holy orders to become a nun, she dedicated her life to revenging Matt's demise. This way she shied away from a lifetime of celibacy and still engaged regularly in affairs of the flesh. The Brits might currently have the upper hand regarding technology but using her computer skills she vowed to bring the Provisional IRA into the modern world.

David Cossar was a successful self-made businessman who used his negotiating skills when attending trade seminars around the world not only to bring work into Northern Ireland but also to hold clandestine meetings with the dark forces who supplied the IRA with weapons. On a more localised front he was constantly back and forward to the Irish Republic and able to arrange a steady supply of illegal drugs (to satisfy Northern Ireland's crack-heads) crossing the border. Michael Caldwell respected what David did for their group but never got too close to him as he secretly disapproved of how he conducted his business and the people he dealt with in his transactions.

A good team, thought Michael as he rose from the table, and one which was extremely capable of keeping the lid on things in Northern Ireland. However, only Mhairi and Colm, as university lecturers were professionally equipped and suited to moving around the world seamlessly, which was essential for Michael to implement Michael's plan of attack.

Chapter 2

MAY 7th 1982

Matt O'Reilly valued his Irish heritage intensely and it was not long before he made contact with the republican movement in Derry offering not only to contribute funds but also to promote fund-raising along the American Eastern Seaboard on their behalf. Born into a rich Irish American family the conversation in the O'Reilly house was often about events in Ireland. When at Harvard Matt became a member of the Bostonian Sinn Fein Club. He had developed into good looking young man with fair hair, hazel eyes and an athletic physique which he put to good use to become a quarterback in the Harvard Football Team. His considerable fund-raising efforts did not go unnoticed by the British authorities who issued a warning from Downing Street - a statement stressing that 'we take an extremely dim view of non-UK dissidents providing funding that results in further mayhem being created in Great Britain.'

Matt chose regretfully to ignore the warning and when he flew into Shannon airport to be met by an IRA deputation instructed to escort him to Derry, he was unaware that his every movement was being monitored. Martin Flynn and his minders who met him at Shannon Airport introduced themselves and provided Matt with the password 'Mick' by way of I.D. clearance before they set off on the two-hundred-mile journey, going north along the N15. The driver announced that he would come off the motorway at Ballybofey, take the N13 to Letterkenny, then enter Northern Ireland by way of a minor road, before approaching Londonderry.

Five miles inside the border Lieutenant Colin Inglis, team leader to three marine snipers specially flown in from SAS headquarters in Hereford, received the news "They've just crossed the border, four occupants in the car, probably armed, including 'the Golden Egg' from Boston who's wearing, would you believe it, a royal blue Ralph Lauren sailing jacket. Apprehend them and show this young man we mean business but do not take him out, repeat DO NOT TAKE HIM OUT!"

The green Range Rover was approaching a bend in the road when the bullet hit the rear onside tyre; "Fuck! A blow-out" screamed Donald Weir, the driver as, he fought to bring the vehicle under control manoeuvring it away from the high wall to the left before coming to a sudden halt. "Everyone out and be vigilant" instructed Martin as his fellow bodyguards revealed their weapons to Matt.

"Hey steady up guys it's only a puncture" exclaimed Matt, trying to bring some calm to the party after the initial shock of seeing guns being produced from nowhere.

"Shut up Yank. Over here you don't get second chances. The Brits delight in entertaining sitting ducks that sneak across the Border" replied Martin, "Flynn, you and Brennan cover my back as I change the tyre".

Martin moved towards the rear of the vehicle, eyes widened at the sight of the bullet-hole in the rear tyre - 'It's an ...'" He didn't get a chance to say 'ambush' when the hail of bullets from the marines' silencer-fitted automatic weapons entered his and the other bodyguards' bodies simultaneously. Matt was left stunned standing in the centre of a bizarre death scene unable to take in how life had been removed silently from his companions whose bodies were now haemorrhaging pools of blood.

Lieutenant Colin Inglis broke his cover, approached the shaken American and in his best Sandhurst accent shouted, "Don't move, my men have you in their sights and have orders to shoot if you make a wrong move."

"You bastards, you shot them in cold blood - what crime have they committed?" yelled O'Reilly.

"Taking money from the likes of you and others like you who have this fantasy about re-uniting Ireland by providing funding to allow this lot to carry out their heinous crimes is monstrous. You don't understand how they control their followers, never allowing their youth to mix with the other half of the population for fear that they actually build up relationships and learn to live in harmony with each other. That would upset the considerable income they accumulate from drugs and protection rackets - not to mention the fall in their selfesteem within the local community."

"That's bullshit!!" exploded the American "we have every right to campaign for the benefit of restoring what we feel is rightfully ours. How can you possibly not agree with me?"

"Oh, I would agree with you - provided that you and your fellow citizens agree to return the United States to the Red Indians," retorted the Lieutenant.

"You smug arrogant English bastard!"

Colin Inglis, sensing he had hit a nerve smirked "Scottish actually"

The Irish anger in the American engulfed Matt's body causing him to search for the nearest weapon which happened to be Flynn's semi-automatic pistol. Diving downwards towards the body he grabbed the gun and attempted to point it towards the lieutenant - a futile move that acted as a catalyst for one of the marines to release a burst of bullets that penetrated the Bostonian's body ending his young life.

A mortified Lieutenant Inglis gasped "God no!! How the hell are we going to explain this to Washington?"

The marine commander had to think quickly on his feet as he had been trained to do, but avoiding international incidents following the cold- blooded murder of an American citizen was not high up on the 'Exceptional Circumstances' manual.

"Christ, what were you thinking about? You knew that our orders were clear that O'Reilly was not to be harmed, so who decided to bring him down?"

The squad looked at each other before Symons raised his hand, "I saw him going for the gun and took action to protect you Sir."

"Ok Symons, thanks, you probably saved my life. Now we have to cover our tracks quickly and, as we have used silencers, nobody has been alerted to our presence. What I want you all to do is, using gloves, fire off some rounds with their weapons and place them back near the bodies. There will an extensive enquiry into this and we shall all be heavily cross-examined by military intelligence so we better make sure that we are all singing from the same hymn sheet. Has anyone any objections to this?"

The marines looked at each other uncomfortably and Inglis sensed trouble ahead.

"Right let's get started before someone drives along. I'll fire off this one" he said reaching down and picking up

Flynn's gun from the side of O'Reilly's body he instructed his team to do likewise. The team moved quickly and fired bursts of gunfire in a semi-circle from the protection of the Range Rover before placing the guns where the bodies had been laid out.

The lieutenant saw his chance and seizing the opportunity turned the Glock on his own squad, who were at ease, guns on the ground and using the surprise element rendered them all dead with a rapid burst of fire. "Sorry lads, but the good name of the Army had to be protected in the face of international media pressure." As well as my military career ambitions, he added mentally.

After quickly ascertaining that they were all dead Inglis radioed in, wiping away the tears, "Emergency! We have apprehended the target but it has all gone horribly wrong –we took out the terrorists but the American got hold off a Glock and sprayed us all killing the squad and wounding me. During the mayhem Symons managed to return fire and killed O'Reilly".

The voice on the other end of the phone responded "We'll get the roads closed off in the next few minutes. A helicopter and back-up will be on their way immediately. Are you badly wounded?"

"No, he caught me on the arm" replied the unscathed soldier.

The call ended, Inglis moved nearer to Matt O'Reilly's body before, using his left hand, firing a shot from the Glock in the direction of his arm forcing him to fall to the ground in excruciating pain. As he fell, his eyes closed, just as there was a rustle in the nearby foliage.

Colin Inglis, the son of a Scottish landowner, had always been 'an awkward boy.' Threatened with his expulsion from a leading public school for bullying, the Inglis family thought his lack of academic achievement may be corrected by army discipline. Colin was admitted to Sandhurst where he continued to show an inconsiderate and arrogant attitude towards his fellow students who referred to him as 'Flashman' after the unscrupulous hero in the George McDonald Fraser novels.

The telephone at IRA headquarters rang and Pat Lafferty the duty officer picked it up. "Derry 2859" he answered.

A voice responded, "Pat, I think we might have a problem. Flynn and two of the boys went down to Shannon this morning to pick up Matt O'Reilly off the Aer Lingus Boston flight. They were supposed to be here over an hour ago but there's no sign of them anywhere. I know the route they were taking and I've had my scouts check it out but they have just vanished."

Lafferty replied with a voice filled with a mixture of anxiety and anger, "Christ this is serious so it is, if anything's happened to O' Reilly I shudder to think of the consequences. Get a hold of his girlfriend Mhairi McClure and see if she's heard from him. Just a minute, stay on the line till I bring up her number on the computer". Lafferty put down the phone and returned thirty seconds later "it's out near Stormont. You'll get her on 899 1213".

It was little wonder that the whereabouts of Matt O'Reilly was unknown as the British helicopter arriving on the scene had witnessed the carnage and

14

immediately arranged for back-up whilst taking control of the situation. The seven dead bodies and the wounded Lieutenant were flown to Masserene Barracks. As it was getting into the air the four occupants who had arrived in the helicopter set about changing the Range Rover's damaged tyre and cleaning up the death scene. Once it was mobile the four removed their helmets and flak jackets before piling into the vehicle and driving at speed for five miles to Muckart Farm where they drove straight into the barn and closed the door and waited until a HGV furniture lorry to arrive. After placing the Range Rover inside the lorry, they set off on the journey back to Army Headquarters.

Chapter 3

"Hi son, did you have a good day?" enquired David Johnston of his son John without lifting his head away from the door he was painting. No reply was forthcoming but that was not unusual for the twelveyear-old.

"I take it you were playing the part of George Best and your pal Hughie was Norman Whiteside, so you won again." Still no reply. David turned, faced the boy and immediately knew something was wrong - tears were streaming down John's face and his young body was shaking.

"What's wrong John?"

"D-D-Dad" the boy stammered, "I was w-walking home when I saw soldiers hiding in the woods and I was scared to move in case they thought I was the enemy. One of them fired a shot at a Range Rover and when the men got out of it they shot them all except one of them who was wearing a blue jacket."

"Why would they do that? Are you sure about this?"

John interjected, taking short breaths to fight back the tears, "Dad that's not all, the man in the blue jacket then picked up a gun and pointed it at one of the soldiers but before he could fire he was shot dead."

"Good God John, come here" comforted David putting his arms round his son, stroking his light brown curly hair, trying to qualm the tremors in his young body. "Let's get you a drink."

David handed John a cup of water which had a calming effect allowing John to relate the rest of what he had witnessed, finalising with Colin Inglis's self-harming.

Johnston senior was by now in a state of shock and his mind was working overtime. He was not doubting what John had told him was genuine but this information was highly dangerous as both sides of the political divide would be out in force, the IRA trying to find out where their men had disappeared to - while the Army would be making sure that they had covered their tracks. John's immediate concern was the safety of his only child, who he had brought up after his wife absconded with her lover and gone off to live in South Africa. As a Protestant, he would be expected to sympathise with the army, but not trusting politicians he had often thought that he could move out of Northern Ireland to ply his trade as an IT engineer elsewhere in the world. His brother Alistair had made the decision to leave 'the Troubles' behind him fifteen years ago and had set up his very successful surveyor practice in Guildford. Married with two children, aged fifteen and ten he had now settled into a Surrey lifestyle.

David sat down directly opposite his son and looking him straight in the eye he commented: "John, I want you to promise me that you will never ever repeat what you have just told me to anyone and that includes especially Hughie." David had long suspected that the parents of his son's friend Hughie McFaul, had links to the Ulster Defence Force. "Today's actions are going to have repercussions and I don't want you to be any part of it. There are evil people out there who will think nothing of harming you to get information. Do you understand what I am saying John?"

The boy, wiping away his tears, nodded his head.

David continued, "This incident has shown me that it is time for us to leave Northern Ireland and settle on the mainland. I can't do this overnight due to work commitments and I wouldn't want to draw any suspicions to us by leaving overnight but I am going to talk to Uncle Alistair and ask him to let you go and live with him. This will take a few days to organise; I will go to your school and explain our departure and how Alistair has fixed you up with a new school. I know you haven't met your cousins Eric and Zoe all that often but you have always got on well and it will only be for a short time until I can sell up here and join you in England. What do you think John?"

"I'll miss all my friends and I don't know if I could stand being English but it is better than going into hiding living with strangers," replied John

David returned his son's smile, "I'll phone Uncle Alistair, you go and have a hot shower and I'll get you something to eat."

Following a very sombre meal that neither of the Johnstons had any stomach for, John said he was going to his room to watch television. After John had left the room David pulled up an A4 pad and prepared his strategy to get Alistair to accept his plan to admit John into his home on a semi-permanent basis. The brothers had been close as children but since Alistair became domiciled in England they had only met up on average every three years.

The phone rang four times in his office before Alistair Johnston picked it up and answered, "Alistair Johnston"

"Hi Al, its David how are things with you?"

Slightly taken aback Alistair responded, "David, long time no hear, good to know you're alive and kicking and still managing to survive in these troubled times."

"You've been reading too many newspapers, things here are not too bad."

"That's not what the television is telling me. There seems to be some concern that an American IRA sympathiser may have gone missing as he has not arrived in Londonderry, after flying into Shannon this morning. In fact, they are suggesting that he may have been passing close by your place."

A shudder passed through David Johnston as he realised the increasing seriousness of what his son had witnessed.

Al continued, "So to what do I owe this phone call?"

"Al, I've got or rather we've got a problem that means that John will have to leave here and settle in England and I would like him to live permanently with you until I can sell up and join him".

"With me? What sort of problem do you have as I can't see me taking him in?"

"I can't explain the problem over the phone but surely you would not turn down taking in your own flesh and blood?" reacted David with anger coming into his voice.

"Easy David, the reason I can't do it is because you will be unaware that Caroline and I have separated - she's got the kids. I had been having an affair with a lady called Judith Duncan and I'm living with her just now until I can move into my own place."

Dejection engulfed David before he answered, "Sorry to hear that Al, you and Caroline always seemed so happy. Well I hope it all settles down and for the sake of the kids you get back together."

"I don't see that happening at present, but I must admit that I'm missing Eric and Zoe. It's a bugger because work wise everything's going well. How about you David?"

"Okay, but I could do with meeting Judith's sister if she has one. Once I have sorted out this little problem I'll meet up with you."

"David, you haven't told me what this problem is, I'll give you any help I can."

"No Al, its better you don't know but thanks anyway - I better go now as I've got more calls to make. Bye for now."

"Bye David" Al responded. "Strange call" he thought, I hope David is not mixed with any of the criminal factions at home.

David stared at the hung-up phone and his A4 pad before scrawling a pen mark across his laid-out strategy. What now? He immediately realised reluctantly that he would have to implement plan B.

The person at the other end of the telephone picked it up and dry mouthed, David began, "Linda, its David and I need your help."

His ex-wife took an aggressive tone: "To what do I owe this pleasure? It must be serious if you need my help".

20

David began nervously to relate the biggest lie he had ever told "John wants to come and stay with you in South Africa. I have got a new girlfriend, Maureen Sinclair, who works in my office and we're intending moving in together. She has two kids and John despises them. The situation has become intolerable and he wants to join his mother in Johannesburg." David continued "Is Claude with you just now?"

"No, he's at the hospital operating" Claude Van Rensburg was a leading neurosurgeon that Linda become involved with when she was an occupational therapist at Londonderry Royal Infirmary, before they decided to move to his South African homeland.

"Yes, I'd love to have him over here and I can make sure he gets a good education. The house has plenty of space and Claude knows it was a wrench for me to leave him in Northern Ireland when we left."

"Don't remind me Linda" David pleaded as he felt tears coming on. "Just go and make arrangements - talk to Claude and see that he is okay with what we want to do and get back to me a.s.a.p. This is unfortunately urgent as John's attitude is causing domestic strife between Maureen and me."

"Claude will be back in 3 hours and I'll phone you back tonight."

"Thanks Linda, talk to you later'."

True to her word Linda rang David back four hours later, "Hello David, I've spoken with Claude and to say our proposal was a shock is an understatement but he is delighted with your suggestion. To let you understand,

and I didn't know this when I left you five years ago, Claude has a low sperm count and is unable to have children of his own. Also, to make the story more credible I had to flower it a little by saying that now John was maturing he had been missing me and you no longer could put up with his tantrums about not seeing me."

"What!" interjected David, "You're still the scheming bitch!"

"I had to" protested Linda, "to give us a good cover for his leaving Ireland and getting into South Africa without any hitches. Claude has contacts in the government, some of his golfing pals at the Wanderers work there, so he's confident it can all be attended to very quickly."
"Is he with you now?" David enquired.

"No, he's gone to play squash with a friend that's why I'm phoning you now"'

David calmed down, "Sorry Linda, my emotions are running off the Richter scale tonight - God knows how I will get on at the airport on John's departure day and if I will be able to cope with life without him."

Linda felt tears in her eyes but managed to blurt out, "David you've always been a good father to John and what I did was wrong, leaving you to bring up a sevenyear-old but we have to put our differences aside for the sake of John's future."

David nodded to himself before replying, "I agree Linda. I will speak to John in the morning and then get back to you with the transport arrangements. Good night and thanks "

Chapter 4

David looked at the steaming kettle whose whistle had awakened him out his deep thoughts on what was going to be one of the most difficult days of his life. John entered the kitchen and sat down at the table. He was dressed in a white and blue hooped jersey over a red polo shirt which brightened up his outfit and made up for the well-worn dull denims that covered his lower half. His Nike trainers completed the look.

"Morning John"

"Morning Dad, how did you get on with Uncle Alistair? Has he got me enrolled for his local rugby team yet?" replied John trying to put a brave face on things and not wanting to start the day recalling the nightmares he had encountered during the night that had affected both his and his father's sleep.

David sat down at the table and began, "John there has been a change of plan. I spoke to Uncle Al last night but he can't help us. I didn't know that he has separated from Auntie Caroline and has moved out of the house in Guildford."

"But what about Eric and Zoe, Dad. What's happening to them?" John enquired.

"I'll come to that - they are staying with their Mum and hopefully sometime in the future they will all get back together again. To continue, as I said yesterday I have to get you away from any bad men bringing harm to you so I had no choice but to phone your Mum last night. I had to lie to her and made up a story that I had taken up

23

with a new partner that you objected strongly to and the situation was so bad that you had asked to go and live in South Africa. John, I had to do this in case the intelligence forces had 'Tapped our phone'."

John's face was one of disbelief, "Johannesburg! But Dad she left us to go off with that doctor and okay she phones once a month but it means I won't see you or my friends. It's not like going to Uncle Alistair's where Hughie or any of the rest of my pals could come over for a holiday."

"I know that son" sympathised his father, "but what you saw yesterday changed everything. It has been on the television that the man in the blue jacket is a member of a rich, powerful Irish-American family who will also be seeking information into his death. They will be just as ruthless as the IRA or British Forces in how they come about that information. From our point of view, it gives us a better cover story that you are going to join your mother rather than us leaving Northern Ireland suddenly that would attract suspicion with the various factions.

I will start making arrangements by, first calling in at your school today and then seeing a travel agent about flights to South Africa. I'll come with you as far as Heathrow and the airline will look after you during the flight and hand you over to your Mum when the plane lands in Johannesburg.

I only met Claude a couple of times and although what happened between your Mum and me angered me, Claude is not a bad person. He has no children of his own so he will look after you. Both Mum and me, despite our past differences, want to ensure your future."

24

John sat silent, trying to take in what his father had just told him. Despite his mother's selfish actions five years ago he did still miss her although the bond to his Dad was much stronger. Thoughts flashed through his head - how often would he see his Dad in the future if ever? How long would it be before he could return to Northern Ireland? Would he be able to make new friends in Johannesburg?

"Dad I'll find it really difficult to live without you but I know you and Mum are only doing what's best for me. What I saw yesterday terrified me and I know that everyone at school will be talking about what they have seen on TV about the men who were shot and I would be scared that I let something slip out accidentally about what happened. I'll go to South Africa."

Chapter 5

Colonel Harper, Head of Army High Command in Londonderry looked over the rimless glasses on the end of his red nose at his assembled strategy team, "Right let's get this damn mess sorted out. I'm under pressure from the PM who's getting it in the neck from the President in Washington, as the O'Reillys' are big donators to his re-election campaign. Robertson, give us a quick resume of what happened."

Captain Ian Robertson, a slim bald figure who, if he had not had the discipline of army life, would probably have been a geek, began:

"F Patrol, three SAS marines under the command of Lt. Inglis, were flown in especially from England and despatched to intercept an IRA vehicle bringing Matt O'Reilly to Londonderry for a funding rally. Our sources tell us that this event was to be publicised to the world media on the completion of the rally - to demonstrate how their campaign for a United Ireland was gaining respectability. Also, it was expected that contributions to their cause, particularly in the USA, would increase dramatically.

Lt. Inglis's orders were to show the realities of life in Northern Ireland to Mr O'Reilly by apprehending the vehicle he was travelling in, killing the occupants, and taking him back to Shannon for the next flight home." "What a load of tosh!" the voice of Warrant Officer Combe boomed out. Eyes turned to the thick-set figure with a full head of speckled grey hair, "Who in their right mind devised that plan, it's like something out of the Wild West rather than West of Ireland. An action of this nature would only strengthen ties between both sides of the Atlantic."

The Colonel responded, "The intelligence services recommended the plan to the MOD and someone up there bought into it."

Combe replied "You mean the lack of intelligence services, Sir."

Colonel Harper gave the Warrant officer a look to kill before nodding at the previous speaker, "Continue Captain Robertson."

Robertson glared at his colleague Combe before going on, "Everything was going according to plan until Lt.

26

Inglis appeared to drop his guard momentarily thereupon Matt O'Reilly seized one of the dead terrorists' guns and sprayed a few rounds killing the three marines and wounding Lt. Inglis, resulting in him losing two fingers of his right hand. The marines had managed to return fire as four bullets were found in O'Reilly's abdomen killing him instantly. Lt. Inglis has been flown to a military hospital in Birmingham for treatment. The incident site was cleared after Lt. Inglis gave the alert and the seven bodies are now at a secret location awaiting instruction."

"Thanks Captain Robertson" said the Colonel, "so what do we do now? The IRA are out looking for their missing 'troopers', reports from Boston say the O'Reillys have sent their attorney/security experts on a plane that is likely to arrive in Shannon in the next few hours. As I see it we have a major dilemma on our hands that can be solved in one of several ways:

Option 1. We admit to what has happened.

Option 2   We don't admit to anything.

Option 3   We contact the IRA through our sources and tell them that we did a routine stop on a Land Rover, the occupants got out the vehicle, panicked and started shooting. We returned fire, killing their men who were led by a man wearing a blue jacket urging them in an American accent to kill 'the British Bastards.'

Option 3 would result in Matt O'Reilly becoming a 'martyr to the cause' and no doubt songs will be written about him both here and in the States. That's the price we have to pay but it is small compared with a charge being laid upon the British Army that we ambushed and slaughtered innocent civilians, that would probably end up with a war crime siting being raised at the Court of Human Rights in The Hague."

Addressing his four colleagues the Colonel looked them all in the eyes before asking, "What do you think?"

The response was unanimous; "Option 3' although W.O. Combe threw in a caveat, "Neither the IRA or the O'Reilly family are to be given Lt. Colin Inglis's name."

    •   •   •   •   •

When Major George Gilzean entered the private ward at Selly Oak Hospital in Birmingham, Colin Inglis was sitting watching county cricket. The Major's presence made Lieutenant Inglis want to stand to attention but the senior officer waved his arm gesturing that he remains where he was.

"Just popped in to do a quick debrief on what happened four days ago,' began Gilzean, 'just to keep the records straight you understand."

"Yes Sir, absolutely", responded Inglis, "would you like some tea?"

Taking a seat Major Gilzean continued, "No, I have to be back home in Oxford in a couple of hours for a dental appointment. Now, let me see, you appear to have been bloody unlucky. Military Intelligences' plan would have worked a treat had it not been for O'Reilly reacting the way he did and taking out three of our finest marines. Tell me, who was it that shot and killed O'Reilly?"

Colin Inglis hesitated before replying, "Everything happened so fast, nobody expected an American sympathiser to react the way he did, but I seemed to recall Symons fired simultaneously as O'Reilly sprayed us with bullets. The men didn't get a chance and I was lucky he responded when he did and managed to survive. I would like Symons to be considered for a bravery award, Sir."

"Yes, I will see that all your men receive recognition for their bravery."

Inglis's face took on a sympathetic smile before replying, "Thank you, Sir"

Looking at Colin's heavily bandaged right hand Major Gilzean asked, "It's the forefinger and middle finger that you've lost isn't it Lieutenant?" "Yes Sir" replied the wounded soldier.

"Unfortunate, this will be an end to your military career in the field, but you are a bright young officer and one who has been noticed by the MOD. They have recommended that you be transferred to Military Intelligence to further your career."

"Thank you, Sir, I was worried that I would have to find something in civvy street to whittle away my time" a relieved Inglis retorted.

"Well I must be on my way" the major said getting out of the visitor's armchair. On reaching the door he stopped and turned, "One thing Inglis, in future be more accurate in your reports, when you radioed in for assistance you said you had been wounded in the arm - not had two bloody fingers removed!"

"I'll bear that in mind Major" replied a red-faced relieved Lieutenant Inglis, cursing under his breath at his potentially lethal gaff.

Chapter 6

Richard Hartley, MI5's top negotiator, flanked by two advisors, stared across the mahogany table in a private room they had hired at the 'Standing Stones' pub in Crossmaglen. Opposite him sat Kieron Toomey his equal in the IRA who was also accompanied by two assistants. Both parties had carried out a sweeping search over the room for electronic bugs that had proved negative. After introductions Hartley read from a prepared statement in front of him:

"We are here today to discuss an incident that occurred on May 7 1982 at 15.30hrs on the road between Inchlong and Londonderry. A Range Rover containing four occupants was waved down and asked to stop by one of our patrols. The vehicle pulled up twenty yards from our patrol and they were ordered to get out of the vehicle so it could be inspected. As they alighted from the vehicle one of the passengers, wearing a blue sailing jacket, appeared to incite the others by crying out in an American accent, 'Let the British bastards have it!' and opening fire. Our men immediately reacted taking out the other three passengers but not before the leader, whom we understand to be Matthew John O'Reilly, mortally wounding the three soldiers also slightly injuring their officer."

Toomey interjected, "O'Reilly was unarmed so how did he manage to shoot anyone?"

Hartley was ready for this question, "He had taken possession of Martin Flynn's automatic weapon.

"Pity he died for his trouble", reacted Toomey, "but we'll see he gets hero's status in our community."

"Gentlemen if I might continue" Hartley asked after taking a sip of water, "Her Majesty's Government regrets what happened especially when Mr O'Reilly's identification became clear. This is an unfortunate accident and one that neither party could have envisaged happening. It was the result of a complete lack of knowledge on Mr O'Reilly's part as to how warfare is conducted in Northern Ireland. We fully expect the IRA to use this incident to their advantage in propaganda both here and in the States where Matthew O'Reilly will no doubt be given a hero's funeral."

Silence filled the room before Toomey began loudly, "So that's it, you expect us to accept this explanation on an incident that has left three of our troops dead and an American supporter going home to Boston in a box! There is some explaining required so there is, where and when did this take place and who was your officer in charge? Did he follow the code of conduct we unofficially agreed for stop and search situations?"

Hartley raised his hand to signal Toomey to cease his outburst before carrying on: "We are prepared to show you where the attack took place so that your forensic staff can judge for themselves what happened but we are, for security reasons, not obliged to disclose the name of our senior officer who survived the attack. Can I remind you gentlemen that the British Army has suffered losses in a routine search due to the actions of a loosecannon American hothead who was in Northern Ireland to support your cause? The next time you invite someone from the United States to Northern Ireland I would advise you to brief them better so that there are no further incidents of this nature"

The others on Hartley's side of the table nodded but their counterparts opposite sat grim faced before Toomey spoke, "Point taken, I will inform my superiors on what you have said and report back their response through our usual channels."

Hartley replied in a relaxed tone, "Thank you for listening to our explanation and we will await your communiqué."

At that both parties rose from the table looked each other in the eye before the republicans headed for the door where their armed bodyguards were ready to escort them to their vehicles, all with false number plates. In a few moments, the vehicles disappeared quietly into the dark overcast night.

Hartley waited until he and his colleagues were in their own car before addressing his men, "Thank God that's over, I'm fed up telling lies on behalf of our army friends. Do you think they bought our explanation?"

Cummings, Hartley's closest confident replied, "Yes for now, but as we know they have long memories so I would not like to be in Colin Inglis's shoes tonight."
Chapter 7

Four weeks later at Heathrow Airport father and son Johnston embraced each other tightly just before John was due to board on Flight SAA 235 to Johannesburg. Holding back the tears David whispered in John's ear, "Remember John, I will always be here for you but today is the start of a new phase in your life that you're Mum and I agree is best for you. Remember our secret and only tell your Mum, not Claude"

John nodded, and then burst out crying "Dad I'll miss you'." As he held John close to him David signalled to the South African Airways stewardess to come forward. Kneeling down to look John in the eyes he said, "This lady will look after you until your Mum meets you at Jan Smuts Airport in Johannesburg." The stewardess smiled, picked up the young boy's hand luggage, placed a reassuring arm gently on his shoulder before leading him off in the direction of the departure gate.

After they disappeared into the departure lounge David completely broke down and sat in a chair sobbing into a hankie for several minutes until he was composed enough to head for the nearest bar for sustenance to help kill the grief.

John and David Johnston were not to know that this was the last time they would see each other alive.

John did not have a good flight and cried a good bit of the way. When he saw his mother waiting for him at Jan Smuts Airport he rushed into her arms and the two of them sobbed for what seemed an eternity. A slightly embarrassed Claude Van Rensburg tapped the new arrival on the shoulder and presented him with a Springboks rugby jersey before saying in a soft Afrikaans accent, 'Welcome to South Africa.'

The next ten days was spent taking John round the Transvaal tourist attractions before going on a four-day safari to the Kruger National Park which John loved.

Claude had returned to work leaving John and Linda sitting round the pool. It was the first time they had been on their own and John took the opportunity to speak to his Mother.

"Mum I've got a secret to tell you."

"And what's the big secret you want to tell me John?" Linda replied expecting some juvenile trivia.

"Dad hasn't got a new girlfriend and I didn't want to come and live in South Africa!'

Linda was shocked by John's secret and immediately went into a rage, "Why are you here then? Claude and I have been prepared to change our whole lifestyle to accommodate you and now you're saying that we have been told a pack of lies!"

John looked at his mother and tears ran down his cheeks, 'Mum it is not like that, Dad is only doing what is right for me after what I saw back home. Let me tell you about it." John then related to his Mum everything about the murders he had witnessed.

When he had finished Linda held her distressed son in her arms, "You poor thing, the ravages of confrontation should never affect children like you. This is our secret and nobody else will know about, not even Claude."
Chapter 8

NOVEMBER 1988

David Johnston was chuffed when he received a call from his control centre on his brand new mobile phone "David, John Clark here, can you arrange to go to Antrim Uni and meet up with a Miss Mhairi McClure, a senior lecturer in computer studies? She has reported that her system is playing up and is concerned that it might be related to an Internet bug, or to give its proper name Morris Worm. This damn virus has been released by some silly boffins from Cornell University carrying out research that has malfunctioned and is causing headaches for everybody."

"I've read about it and as long as we can get to it promptly I should be able to sort it out" responded David.

"Okay then, I'll leave it in your capable hands. Here's the number for Miss McClure."

David wrote down the number then killed the previous call before dialling the numbers on his notepad. After two rings the person on the other end picked up the phone:

"Mhairi McClure speaking, how can I help you" the soft voice asked.

"Oh, Miss McClure it's David Johnston from N.I. Computer Solutions my boss John Clark asked me to phone as I understand you have a problem with your system and I want to know when it is convenient to come in and resolve it?"

"Well that's quick service, I only phoned five minutes ago. Mr Johnston, I would be delighted to see you soon as possible."

"I'm about five miles away from you at present finishing off a job so I can be there in about an hour and a half."

"Excellent Mr Johnston, when you come into the University Quadrant ask the security guard on the gate to direct you to Computer Studies. You'll find us on the second opening on the left. Look forward to meeting you Mr Johnston."

"Likewise, Miss McClure - and by the way my friends call me David."

David's grey van with its blue trimmings entered Antrim Uni campus and pulled up at the gatehouse barrier opposite a glass bulletproof window with a grill through which he announced, "I'm here to see Miss McClure at Computer Studies."

The guard responded, "Just a minute Sir."

There was a thirty second delay whist he made a call to Computer Studies, allowing his colleague to walk round the van with a metal detector. He then handed him a white disc telling him he must wear it at all times.

David parked the van, got out his toolkit, entered the building and headed for reception but before he reached there a voice from behind called out, "Are you Mr Johnston, sorry David?"

David turned and was startled to find that coming towards him was Miss McClure, a young attractive blonde woman wearing a light blue blouse and a grey straight skirt and twiddling a pair of horn-rimmed spectacles in her left hand. After handshakes Mhairi led the way to her office - a substantial high ceilinged room that housed her desk behind which was a high-backed rocker chair on wheels, facing the two visitor seats positioned in front of the desk. The walls were lined with books and magazines interrupted only by a cabinet that was adorned with two crystal decanters and six glasses.

Mhairi sat down behind the desk and told David to pull up a chair. She began, "I only noted the problem this morning when I tried to retrieve some data that had been sent to us from America. As you can imagine we think that we are secure but we were getting malware warnings and so I took the precaution to phone NICS. My computer controls all the sensitive data on the system, so if there is anything else you need just ask.

David smirked, "A cup of coffee and a chocolate biscuit won't go far wrong."

Mhairi returned his smile, "any particular chocolate biscuit?' "A Kit Kat please"

Ten minutes later a lady appeared with a jug of coffee and the requested biscuit. By this time David had ensconced himself in front of the computer and using his own bag of tricks to carry out tests that allowed him to narrow down the problem. The Morris Worm was very new but NICS prided itself with making their engineers aware of developing problems so David was fairly confident that he would solve the problem although it would take patience.

After almost two hours David satisfied himself that the University system was 'clean' but decided to run the systems one last time which he estimated would take about ten minutes. His concentration levels having reached exhaustion he now relaxed and toured the room looking at Miss Mhairi McClure's qualification certificates and the photographs on the wall.

One in particular caught his attention, a young smiling fair-haired man in a green polo shirt with the message:

To Mhairi,

The love of my life and soon to be my wife.

Love Matt xx

The penny suddenly dropped. David knew the face staring him was that of Matt O'Reilly the man whose presence had changed his life by forcing him to be separated from his only son.

A bleep from the computer indicated an end of checklist procedures so David returned and sat in front of the machine. His head was buzzing at the discovery on the wall and his curiosity made him open the drawers of the desk and look inside. The top right-hand drawer contained personal effects associated with most ladies but in the bottom drawer there were a number of computer discs all carefully labelled concerning all the various university departments. David lifted out the box and as it reflected on the computer screen he saw that there was a yellow labelled disc sellotaped to the bottom of the box. By now his heart was racing, as he prised the disc from its hiding place and placed the yellow saucer into the computer. Instantaneously a heading appeared on the screen:

THE 1972 CLUB

1. Constitution.

2. Members

3. Minutes

4. Funding

David opened the file and immediately felt a shiver down his back as he realised that he was looking at the working papers of a major IRA cell and one that would think nothing of eliminating anyone who infiltrated their gang. Realising the importance of the data David inserted one of his own discs and began to copy the data. His hands started to shake and his pulse was racing by the time his disc finished copying and ejected the original disc. The engineer re-fastened the disc back to the secret hiding place and was still taking deep breaths when the door opened and Mhairi waltzed in "How's it going?" she asked.

"All sorted Miss McClure. I don't think you'll be needing to call me back again. I've just finished all the data checks and I was admiring your qualifications up there on the wall." he said gesturing towards the hanging frames. "The young man in the green shirt is that your boyfriend?"

"My fiancée actually, Matt was killed by the British forces a number of years ago" a despondent Mhairi replied.

"Oh, sorry to hear that. I remember that incident when an American fellow in a blue jacket died alongside soldiers and IRA sympathisers."

 Mhairi was taken aback by David's memory detail. How could he possibly know that Matt had been wearing the blue Ralph Lauren jacket she had given Matt for his birthday as the jacket had gone missing when Matt's body was taken to the morgue at Masserene?

40

"Oh, that was a number of years ago and life has to go on. How about you David, are you rushing home to the wife now?"

"No, she's long gone - what I mean is we separated years ago. I'm meeting my pals in 'The Last Drop' for a few drinks tonight. Being Friday I'll probably get pissed - sorry drunk."

Mhairi put on her best smile, "Well, have a good night and thanks again. Have you got a card in case I want to contact you in the future?"

With shake of the hands and David having provided his business card, he left the room, leaving Mhairi deep in thought. She looked up at Matt's photo and suddenly became uncomfortable. David Johnston had proved in the last few hours to be a sophisticated computer engineer but also one who appeared to have considerable knowledge of what went on in his community. Mhairi opened her right –hand drawer and saw that her box of discs was where she had left it but on closer examination discovered that the disc which she had stuck down with a double layer of sellotape flopped away from the bottom of the box when she lifted it out of her drawer.

"Shit!!" she screamed internally, "that bastard has been into the 1972 Club Files and has probably copied them and is on his way to see the Royal Ulster Constabulary (RUC)."

Picking up the phone she dialled the Chancellor's office. A voice answered "Chancellor's phone, can I help you" It was Michael Caldwell's PA Margot.

41

"Its Mhairi McClure here, is Michael available?"

"No, he's tied up at a Students Union meeting and won't be free for another hour or two."

"Can you interrupt him? It is vital I speak to him as soon as possible", Panic was now setting in as Mhairi began to contemplate the serious nature of her discovery.

Margot replied, "Sorry Mhairi, but this is a very important meeting to decide budgets for the next two years and the Chancellor said that under no circumstances is he to be interrupted."

"Okay, okay" Mhairi stammered looking at her watch, "so he should be free around six p.m. Can you put a red star on the message when you leave it on his desk as I must speak to him this evening?" "Yes, I will." the PA confirmed.

"Thanks Margot. Have a good weekend."

One hundred minutes later Mhairi's phone rang," 'Hi Mhairi, Michael here, what's so important that you are still in your office at this time on a Friday?"

"Michael, are you alone and your phone's not on loudspeaker, is it?"

"No, only me and a large Scotch. You sound anxious what's wrong?"

Mhairi related the afternoon's events climaxing in her fear that David Johnston had copied their secret file. Michael felt stress steeping through his body and he expelled a long breath partially to allow him time to analyse the situation.

He began: "What do we know about this Johnston character? Where he goes and how big a threat is he?"

"I have his contact details as he left me his card. He's separated from his wife but I don't know if he has any family. He was a bit of a charmer in his own way but I got the impression that the wife had left him as he mentioned meeting his mates at a pub called 'The Last Drop' where he goes to get drunk."

Michael butted in, "That's fine - the 'Last Drop' is out near Stormont Prison. It's an old pub opened when hanging was still in operation, thus the name. Mhairi, we will have to treat this as a Red Alert so I'll inform the rest of the committee and decide on a course of action. We can't take a chance that Johnston has not been in touch with the authorities so PK will have a hit squad in place immediately. I'll get Seamus Carr to get one of his surveyors into the pub and start talking to Johnston to see where he has been since he left your office."

"Good Michael, as always I'll leave this side of the business to the men. Keep me informed of developments." "Will do. Goodnight."

Carol Knight and Lizzie Waugh both dressed up for a night out, with plunging necklines, short skirts and high heels opened the door of the Last Drop, carrying on a conversation as they did so, not to attract the stares of the customers. Lizzie approached the bar and a short time later ordered a vodka and a dark rum both with diet cokes. The bar was busy, with piped music playing and the customers all appeared generally happy. Carol surveyed the clientele as Lizzie paid for the drinks. She spotted Johnston, whom she recognised by the

43

description given by Mhairi McClure, sitting at a table with two mates ten yards right of where they were standing. He stood out from the others by his lack of sartorial elegance compared with his colleagues. With their drinks in hand the girls edged towards earshot of the Johnston table and a quick smile in the direction of the men drew an immediate reaction.

"Well ladies, to what do we owe this pleasure. I'm Jimmy Slater, 'Roofer' to my mates and this is Tommy O'Hagen, the well-built dark haired handsome one. "Tommy raised his glass by way of identifying himself. Both men were in their mid to late thirties and the smaller Tommy had long ago traded his fair locks for a skinhead.

The girls said "hello" before Lizzie asked "And who's your pal? Does he not have a name?"

David stared at the women through hazy eyes then returned to his drink.

"This is David Johnston, our computer whizz kid who is a little worse for wear tonight. The barman said he came in here straight from work which is not really like him. He's usually dressed to kill and sees himself as Stormont's answer to George Clooney, isn't that right Davie." Roofer concluded.

David looked up and communicated through slurred vocal chords, "Shorry ladies, I've had a bad day that brought back a lot of bad memories of the time when my wife left me taking my son with her."

The girls looked at each other, nodded to each other in acknowledgement that they had reached their target.

Then Carol enquired, "Will you be okay for getting home? Do you live locally?"

David moved his lips to respond but it was Tommy's voice they heard, "He lives in Palmerston Place about half a mile away but don't worry girls he'll make it home. He's managed every other Friday night. Where are you off to yourselves?"

"Oh, we're off to a hen party in the town we just popped in for a wee starter."

"That's a pity, Roofer and I could have shown you a good time."

Lizzie downed her drink before saying, "Come on, Carol the girls will be wondering where we are. Thanks for the offer Tommy and who knows we might catch up with you another time."

Once they were outside the pub the girls hailed a taxi that had been waiting nearby. The driver asked where they were going before pulling away, turning the corner before stopping three hundred yards up the road. The driver turned his silver-hair head to face the girls and they immediately realised their reconnaissance was of the highest importance as facing them was 'PK' who was not a man to be treated lightly.

"Did you meet Johnston?"

Carol reported, "Yes sir, and he is definitely getting stuck into the booze because as he says 'he's had a bad day that reminded him of when his wife left him'. Sad case really."

"Well I'm not a domestic councillor. Tell me what's he wearing?"

Lizzie took a turn at answering, "He's got on his work uniform, that's dark grey trousers and shirt but he's got a navy-blue V-neck on top of it. He had a navy-blue jerkin on the seat beside him that also had NICS logo on it."

"Thanks girls you've been very useful. I'll stay on here," PK said reaching into his pocket, "Here's £100 for your trouble. Now go and get a taxi."

It was nearly another two hours before David came out, or rather stumbled out of the pub with Roofer and Tommy.

PK slumped down in his seat and wound down the window of the Mondeo so he could hear the group's conversation.

"Davie, we're heading for the clubs to see if these two lassies we met earlier and the rest of the hen party are looking for company." Roofer shouted.

"Besht of luck boys", David slurred, "ahm off home for a nightcap."

"Will you be all right Davie"' Tommy asked.

"No need to worry about Davie boy, Tommy. After what I witnessed today I could have all the protection in the world if I wanted it."

"Okay then we'll see you in the pub tomorrow before we go to the football."

PK watched as David swayed his way up the road for two hundred yards before turning into Palmerston Place a quiet but broad street of bungalows each with their own driveway so there was not much in the way of parked cars.

David had moved into the city after John had left for Johannesburg. PK followed and after turning the corner planned his assault. Checking to see there were no cars around he revved up the engine, set off at speed and mounted the kerb. David saw the path illuminate in front of him and turned to see the glare of headlights just before the car hit him. His body catapulted forward and lay motionless until PK ran over his body to make sure his task was complete. PK quickly jumped out the car and confirmed his target dead before driving off at speed. As he looked in his rear mirror shadows were appearing from the houses to examine the carnage he had left behind. He doubted if anyone had time to record the vehicle number plate not that it mattered as it was false and the car had been stolen earlier in the day.

PK drove carefully into an industrial estate in East Belfast and straight into O'Halloran's scrapyard. He quickly changed his shoes and, without removing his gloves, placed them in the cabin of the Mondeo. Above him a crane appeared and the driver guided the claws of his vehicle through the Mondeo's windows before loading it on to a crusher where, within minutes, it had been had reduced to a square cube of waste metal. Once the remnants of the Mondeo were released from the crusher the crane completed the task by uplifting the metal cube and placing it on a low loader, which was immediately dispatched to Larne. From there it was transferred on to a ship which was heading for the Belgian port of Zeebrugge in the morning.

An hour later PK was back home and telephoned Michael Caldwell, "Mission completed" was all he said and replaced the phone on the hook.

Michael Caldwell looked at his watch before phoning Mhairi. It was after midnight but he still dialled her number. Three rings and she answered.

"Michael here Mhairi, sorry to phone so late, but I just wanted you to get a good night's rest. PK phoned - Mr Johnston will not be troubling you again."

"Thanks, that's a relief." she exhaled, "He really had me worried. Goodnight Michael."

Mhairi put down the phone and briefly contemplated the result of her actions but then balanced any grief by thinking how she had been wronged when Matt was assassinated. The irony of the evening was that she had played her part in liquidating the only man in Northern Ireland who knew the truth about her fiancée's death.

Inspector Liam Cranston arrived at Palmerston Place to be met by an all too familiar scene which after twentyfive years in the police felt like a normal day at the office. Blue tape cordoning off the crime scene, several police officers guarded the incident area and his old friend Eric Calder plus his forensic team were gathering up vital information. Turning to his sergeant Claire Allan he said, "Okay, let's find out what this is all about."

Creeping up behind the forensic scientist Cranston said in a loud voice, "Evening Eric, what's your initial thoughts?"

The diminutive scientist was startled and turned to face Cranston, "Oh I might have guessed it was you Liam. Well it's not adding up yet so I think you will have to do some digging to get a result. Basically, it appears to be a hit and run resulting in the victim David Johnston's death, but it's not the normal Friday night drink driver accident."

"Why do you say that Eric?"

'Well, the victim was not only hit from behind at speed but driven over by his assailant to make sure he didn't survive. Footprints we have found near the body suggests the culprit then appears to have got out of his vehicle to make sure Johnson was dead before driving off at speed."

"Thanks Eric" the inspector said before turning to Claire Allan, "Anything come through on the victim?"

"Yes - David Johnston (41), divorced, one son John who lives with his mother in South Africa. His next of kin in this country is his brother Alistair who lives in Surrey. David was a computer engineer with a local firm in Belfast.

Apparently, he had been drinking heavily in the 'Last Drop' with a couple of friends but had left them to make his own way home. He has been described as 'a nice lad' and checks out that way, he is not a member of any political party and spent his spare time going to football or fishing. He was very attached to his son and was upset

49

when the boy wanted to go and live with his mother. That was over six years ago and he has never been over to South Africa once to see him although he made regular phone calls."

"Well that rules out any spurned lover. Claire get his two mates in for questioning in the morning and we'll see if we can paste anything together. I'll speak to his employers to get a picture of his movements. Not much more we can do here tonight. C'mon let's go home."

Linda Van Rensburg was relaxing with a book on the patio of her luxurious villa in the Rivonia district of Johannesburg when the phone rang. She didn't rush to answer it as she knew her maid Jane would, which proved correct and waited for Jane's entrance. "Madam, it's for you - a Mr Alistair Johnston."

Linda moved briskly to the phone in the hall, "Hello Alistair, this is a surprise, are you holidaying in South Africa with the family? Because if you are Claude and I would be delighted to have you over for a meal and -

Alistair interjected at this point, "Linda, I'm phoning from the UK with some very bad news." There was a silence before he continued in a broken voice, "Its David he's dead."

"David... Dead... How!" Linda screamed.

"We haven't got all the details yet but he appears to have been the victim of a hit and run accident. He had been drinking heavily in The Last Drop not far from his house and had left two friends to stagger home but he hadn't stumbled into the road, it was a car that mounted the pavement and killed him."

Linda slumped against the wall tears now welling in her eyes as Jane placed a seat beside her as she attempted to speak. "Al, Alistair, sorry I'm speechless. Have the police arrested anyone for the accident?"

"No, not yet but they will keep us informed. Being a sudden death I don't know when the funeral will take place but I will keep you posted on developments. Give my regards to John, this will come as a horrendous shock to him. Bye for now."

"Bye Alistair". Linda mumbled gently before the enormity of the call sunk in and her body started to shake as floods of tears cascaded down her cheeks.

Jane was concerned for her mistress, who always treated her very well, but was unsure what to do, as she had never seen the Madam cry before. She plucked up courage to ask, "What's wrong Madam? Is there anything I can do to help?"

Linda lifted her head and blew her nose before answering in a wavering voice, "It's John's dad, my first husband, he's been killed in an accident in Northern Ireland by a hit and run driver."

"Oh Madam, that's shocking. My prayers go out to you and John. I have seen his photograph on John's bedside table so I know how fond he was of his father."

Linda replied, "Thanks Jane, if you could leave me now to think how I should break the news to John."

Linda had to wait a couple of hours before the front door burst open and John Johnston began, "Hi Mum, I'm home" shouted JJ (as John was known to his friends) from the entrance hall, "and wait to you hear how I scored three tries for Jeds (King Edward VII School) to beat Pretoria College 24 -15 and was man of the match! How about that then?"

The usual parental support was not forthcoming and John began to wonder if his Mum was at home. A noise behind him made him turn to face the sad face of the maid, "Madam is out on the patio and she needs to talk to you."

John found his mother with her head buried in a large tissue and as she looked up the red rings round her eyes revealed her grief.

"What's wrong Mum?"

His mother stood up and extended her arms and embraced her boy. "I've had bad news. Uncle Alistair phoned and" her body shivered before she blurted out, "your Dad's been killed in a road accident. No, not a road accident. He was killed by a hit and run driver not far from the house!"

John felt his knees buckle and the sudden desire to vomit which he managed to control before retracting himself from his mother's grasp and circulating the room.

"Dead, how do you mean dead? Dad can't die. We had plans to meet up next year during my gap year." John slumped into a chair and the full impact of his grief exposed itself as he wailed and shed bucket loads of tears before stammering out, "When do we leave for Belfast?"

Chapter 9

Two weeks had passed by the time a large crowd had gathered at Stormont Parish Church to say farewell to David Johnston and welcome the cortege which was followed by two official cars, one of which was occupied by John Johnston, his mother and Uncle Alistair accompanied by his wife Caroline, with whom in the interim he had been reconciled.

The Rev. George Mackay led the mourners in prayers and gave a resume of David Johnston's life before calling upon John to pay a tribute to his father.

The eighteen-year-old approached the microphone on the lectern as the congregation murmured amongst themselves, taking in the change in John whom they had not seen for six years. The wee boy they knew had now become an athletic six foot two man. John was dressed in a smart lightweight navy-blue suit with a white shirt and the obligatory black tie, which complemented his tanned complexion framed by a mane of blond hair bleached by the Transvaal sun. John cleared his throat before commencing in a clipped South African accent:

"Ladies and Gentlemen, on behalf of my family I would like to thank you for your attendance today. Today is a sad one for the Johnston family, Dad was the last person one ever thought would have his life terminated in what looks like a planned assassination. What a waste of a good man whose only ambition was to see me succeed in life. When I made the decision that I wanted to go to Johannesburg to live with my mother who is here with me today, he allowed me to go as he thought it was best for me in the long term. It was a tough decision for him to take and he was looking forward to coming out to South Africa to visit us later this year. I will miss his guidance and our football matches - Dad always played the part of Pat Jennings but made sure I always won by letting me be George Best."

The gathering responded with a chuckle.

"My comments on the nature of my father's death might surprise some of you, but I have the advantage over you of living out with the Province and observing the futility of the actions of the warring factions. I realise that the separation imposed on young people in this community by the political leaders of both sides of the religious divide is particularly damaging as I now attend school with boys and girls of all faiths. British people are quick to cast slurs on the apartheid regime that I now live in but as a friend of my step-father communicated to me, "in South Africa we are split on racial grounds whereas in the UK you choose to destroy each other using religion as your clarion call."

"My ties to Northern Ireland have now been terminated and sadly I will not be the last young person to turn his back on their roots. I hope that the authorities bring the culprits of Dad's death to justice, and that they are given an opportunity to confess to their crimes but absolution be refused to them."

An air of embarrassed silence fell upon the assembled mourners before John concluded, "Mum and I would like to thank you all for your attendance today"

John slowly walked back to his seat and the local minister brought the service to a conclusion by blessing the soul of David Johnston before the coffin was carried out the church to begin its journey to a private service at a local crematorium.

Before they left for the crematorium the Johnston family lined up and shook hands with the well-wishers who had come to pay their respects to David.

John did not know the attractive lady who pressed his flesh but Mhairi McClure had wanted to make his acquaintance, "Hello I'm Mhairi McClure. Your father had fixed my computer system only hours before his death and on behalf of Antrim University I would like to offer my condolences. When did you last speak to your father?"

John replied, "The Sunday before he died, He called me every Sunday."

"We'll all miss him. Please express our sorrow to your family." Mhairi concluded as she turned away relieved that David Johnston had not phoned his son after he left her office the Friday before he met his death.

The wake was held at David Johnston's masonic club where relatives and friends who had not clapped eyes on each other for a long time exchanged stories about David and how their own families were getting on. John politely exchanged pleasantries with the older members of the family but was delighted when his close pal Hughie McFaul caught his eye and indicated that they should go outside for some light relief from the older generation.

"Thanks Hughie for getting me away from Mrs Desmond, she would do your head in with all her questions."

Hughie smiled as he took out a cigarette which he lit before exhaling, 'She means well and would like to get her only daughter married off to a rich South African!'

They both burst out laughing and John continued "You must be finishing school soon Hughie, what do you fancy doing then?"

"Oh, I'm off to Uni, I've got a place at Durham where I'll be doing geography with computer science. Yourself?"

"We do an extra year in South Africa but I hope to go to Stellenbosch where I'll do medicine - and hopefully play a bit of rugby."

"So, you've taken up the oval ball. What happened to' the budding Georgie Best?"

"I go to a private school in Johannesburg, King Edward V11. It's a prominent rugby playing academy. I'm the star fly-half." John informed Hughie with a glint in his eye.

"You always were a cocky bastard", said Hughie, "Come on let's get back to the food."   Chapter 10

The telephone connected to the outer gate at 210 Du Plessis Avenue rang and was answered by Claude Van Rensburg's gardener Thomas, "Hello, how can I help you?", he enquired.

"It's Rennies Delivery Service, I have a parcel for a John Johnston from a David Johnston in Northern Ireland."

Hitting the entry button Thomas replied, "Okay, come up to the house."

After signing for the box Thomas looked at it closely, smiled sadly when he saw the sender was David Johnston and that the content of the parcel was 'Football Boots'.

A week later John and his mother returned to Johannesburg and were met at the airport by Claude who was relieved to see them since the South African press were reporting daily the atrocities in Northern Ireland. As they got in the car heading back to Rivonia Claude enquired "Did everything go okay?"

Linda turned from looking out of the window and sadly said, "As well as could be expected. David's friends and family turned out in force to give him a good send-off but the police are no nearer finding the reason for his killing. I just don't understand it but there again I was never one for conforming to the philosophies of some religious fanatics of either persuasion."

John had been sitting quietly in the back of the car and his demeanour concerned Claude as he observed him in the rear mirror. "You all right John?"

"Yes, just tired after sitting trussed up for 12 hours in economy class."

Rivonia was another world away from Belfast with its rows of white mansions all with their swimming pools and manicured lawns populated by the professional and business classes of Jo'burg who all housed their black servants in quarters at the foot of the garden. The hypocrisy and racial divide shown by the upper class concerned John but he much preferred the life he had now to the one he had left in Northern Ireland.

Jane and Thomas were delighted that Linda and John had returned. After they had unloaded their luggage the family relaxed in the lounge. The tranquil setting was brought to an end by Jane entering the room carrying the package that had arrived the previous week. Her bottom lip trembled as she spoke. "Master John, this is for you. It is from your father."

John jumped out of his seat and accepted the parcel from Jane, staring at it before tears of grief filled his eyes. "I'll open it in my room if you don't mind." Both his South African parents nodded their approval.

After removing the brown packaging John held the red and white football boots in his hand then noticed there was a letter sellotaped to the insole of the right boot.

He recognised his father's writing and ripped open the envelope and began reading:

"Hello John

I hope this letter finds you well and that the boots bring you many hours of happiness on the playing fields although from what you have said recently you are now favouring the oval ball. I am looking forward to coming out to see you later this year and maybe see the boots in action.

Events in Northern Ireland are not getting any better and you are in a better environment in which to plan your future. Inside the left boot I have placed a computer disc that you should only open if in the event of the dark forces eliminating me. Open it in the presence of Linda and Claude as it contains information on some of the people responsible for you moving to South Africa. Hopefully nothing will happen and we will meet again soon.

Look after your mother.

Dad."

John burst into uncontrollable tears followed by screaming obscenities "Bastards! Bastards! They killed my father!" he roared and his grief alerted his parents who rushed into his bedroom to see what was wrong.

Linda picked up the letter from John's bed and seconds later she also began wailing as she held her son tightly to her body. Claude couldn't understand what was going on until Linda loosened her grip on the letter and passed it to him to scrutinise. Claude was aghast at what he had just read and placed his strong arms round both Linda and John creating a bonding huddle that lasted several minutes. When they broke up Claude slid his hand into the left boot and pulled out the silver disc and all three stared at it in fear of its contents.

John broke the silence, "Dad must have bought the boots the day he died and knew that he had uncovered something that was not for his eyes. Rather than be caught with the evidence, he has sent it over to us on the basis that it would never be opened. Someone knew he had it and ordered his execution. So, what do we do now Papa?" asked John of Claude.

"Let's go into my office and I will open this" said Claude referring to the disc he held between his fingers.

Linda instructed Jane to make some coffee while Claude set up his computer and asked not to be disturbed until they had finished their meeting in the Master's study. Claude placed the disc into the computer and it whirred into action causing the screen to flutter before it settled with the headline 'The 1972 CLUB'.

For the next hour, the trio screened through the contents of the disc that gave up all sorts of information - some of which was very confidential and would be of great interest to enemies of the IRA. In one section, there was a report regarding the assassination of Matt O'Reilly that made John glance at his mother who slowly shook her head as a signal not to reveal their secret to Claude. The detail of the file was such that they scanned through much of the financial information and soon brought the viewing to an end.

Claude leaned back in his high-backed office desk chair before stretching his arms. "This is a hot piece of intelligence and explains why David met his untimely end. It is unlikely that this would be traced to ourselves but nevertheless, as a precaution, I think we should try and get some protection. I know a man who will be very interested in this disc and who would be able to supply us with security. Is it alright with both of you if I have a word with him?"

"Yes, yes, by all means" were the reactions of Linda and John.

"Very well I will set up a meeting with Stanley Laab" confirmed Claude.

The veranda of the Wanderers Golf Club, although busy with golfers and diners was large enough for Claude Van Rensburg and Stanley Laab, to find a quiet corner. Laab was a trim fifty-five year-old electronics engineer who ran a printed circuit plant in the East Rand. Of slim build, his thin face below hair receding at the sides sported dark brown piercing eyes that were enhanced by rimless spectacles on a classic Jewish nose.

"That was a good tussle' said Claude, 'I thought you had me with that birdie on sixteen but the two in the bunker at the eighteenth let me square the game."

"Don't remind me, man" said a woeful Laab, "I'll not be so magnanimous next time."

Claude looked over his shoulder before going on, "Stan, I have a private matter I wanted to discuss with you. Are you still making regular business trips to Jerusalem via New York and Geneva?"

Stan looked up, "Yes, but what is that to do with you - I am not involved with the medical profession."

"But you do get involved with security services and have contacts in Mossad, the Israeli intelligence service."

"That is not for discussion." Laab reacted angrily, "I don't know how you can expect me to answer such a question and anyhow why are you even bringing up the subject of Mossad with me?"

Claude felt embarrassed to have jangled a nerve of his golfing companion but pressed ahead in an attempt to get protection for his family. "I am sorry to be so forward but if you will take time to let me explain hopefully we can take this conversation further."

"Okay, carry on" signalled Stan as he was known to his friends.

Within a short time, Claude outlined all that had happened in Belfast and how they had come to be in possession of the disc containing vital IRA data. When he finished Stan Laab sat back in his seat, clasping his hands in prayer fashion and looking to the skies for guidance before he spoke:" 'Where is the disc now Claude?"

Claude put his right hand into the left inside pocket of his light-blue safari jacket "Here."

Stan Laab's eyes lit up, "This is getting like a scene from a Graham Greene novel. So, Harry Lime, what do you want in return? "

"Protection at all times for my wife Linda and her son John wherever they travel throughout the world."

Stan wheezed out a blast of air, "Now that is a big ask. This information better be as good as you say it is. I will pass it on to the appropriate authorities and report back to you. I can't be fairer than that at this stage."

Passing the disc, which he covered with a Wanderer's Club napkin, to his golfing partner, Claude nodded "Understood"

A month passed before Claude received a call from Stan Laab, "Hello Claude, I have received a call from our mutual friends that I would like to discuss with you."

"That's good news Stan. When and where would you like to meet?"

"How would you like a game at The River Club? I have

been given two complimentary vouchers from one of my largest clients."

Claude responded, "Must be a good client as not many people get to play on Schlesinger and Oppenheimer's private golf course."

"You're talking to a man of influence Claude", joked Stan, "I will go ahead and book a tee time. Would this Friday morning suit you?"

Claude glanced at his wall planner before replying, "Yes, perfect. I am not operating until Friday night."

"Okay, see you then"'

Claude stopped his car in front of the electric gates at the entrance to The River Club in the plush area of Sandton. A black security guard n leaned out of the window of his gatehouse and asked Claude to identify himself before opening the gates allowing him to proceed towards the clubhouse. 'The Clubhouse' was not like those at other golf clubs, more like someone's large private house with its thatched roof and veranda.

Stan was waiting for him and escorted him through to the lounge, and he had no sooner settled into an armchair when a waiter seemed to appear out of nowhere and take their order. Both men settled for coffee which they consumed over pleasantries about how it must be nice to have your own private golf course before making their way out on to the course where they met their caddies for the day.

On their way down the par 5 third hole Stan opened up a new topic of conversation: "My command in Tel Aviv were most interested in your disc and have agreed with your request for protection for your family. You will understand this is not an easy service to provide without actually living in your house. What we will do is monitor suspects coming into South Africa whom we see as a threat to your family. When either your wife or son go overseas they must inform us so that we can offer protection without them being aware of it."

"The Israeli government has been starved of a supply of weapons in recent years as has South Africa due to their apartheid policy, and this has led to coalition known as 'the Bastard States' which also includes Chile and other despots round the world. These countries now trade closely amongst themselves. This was not always the case as Israel was also against apartheid but needs must and in 1976 the two countries signed a co-operation treaty. South Africa is blessed with an abundance of raw materials including yellow uranium to make nuclear weapons but lack the know-how, that Israel supplies. I have electronics engineers who come over from Jerusalem to my factory and design professional printed circuit boards that are used for armaments.

The IRA have been funded by Libya for years and Colonel Gadaffi is unlikely to change his stance as he despises the
West for not having a more aggressive condemnation of Israel's actions towards Palestine. The British have a major headache in Northern Ireland so we will hang on to that disc and use it as a bargaining tool at the appropriate moment."

Claude smiled in relief before exclaiming, "Thanks Stanley, can't imagine how happy that makes me feel. I realise it's not fool-proof but gives me considerable piece of mind."

Stan reacted," Well now that's out the way let me concentrate on giving you a good cuffing at golf."
Chapter 11

JUNE 2nd 1998

The University Staff Conference (USC) being held at Aston University in Birmingham attracted academics from all over the UK anxious to explore the latest educational aids to assist their daily task of tutoring the nation.

Two days prior to the start of the conference Michael Caldwell had invited Colm Murphy and Mhairi McClure to his Victorian mansion on the outskirts of Ballymoney for a meal to supposedly discuss their attendance at the USC.

Mhairi and Colm arrived in the former's Mercedes Cabriolet, both in casual clothes, carrying brief cases containing their papers for the conference. Michael had heard their approach and was at the front door, accompanied by his border collie, Luke, to greet them by the time they had got out of their car.

"Good evening and welcome", he voiced impersonating David Frost, "I hope you're not expecting a Michelin meal as my wife has gone over to see her sister in Amersham for a few days so the microwave will be working overtime tonight. But come in and make yourselves comfortable."

The visitors both patted Luke as they filed past Michael into a large oak panelled hall decorated with paintings that were a mixture of rural scenes and sea landscapes with one exception - a portrait of a young boy playing with his dog. Colm and Mhairi knew not to comment on it as was of Michael's only son, Sean, who had been killed when he had stepped out in front of a British Army patrol vehicle speeding to a disturbance in Londonderry.

"In to your right, we'll use the kitchen so that we can spread out our papers and that way I'll never be far from the cooker. Colm, you know where the drinks are. There's beer and spirits in abundance - and I've put a couple of good bottles of Chardonnay in the fridge to go with the fish pie."

The kitchen was spacious as you would expect from a Victorian home, with a large wooden table with eight chairs around it dominating the centre of the kitchen. Wooden oak wall cupboards surrounded the room, only interrupted by a large AGA on one wall.

"Let's get the conference business over first. Then there's something I would like to pass by both of you. Right Mhairi, you tell me what you're looking for at the USC?"

For the next hour, the trio discussed over drinks, what they hoped to achieve in Birmingham and how their departments could benefit from the programme the USC had laid out. A plan of how they could make best use of their limited time to attend the various lectures was agreed so that they each knew what their role consisted of. Having decided their strategy Michael called a halt and suggested they retire to the sitting room while they waited for the food to cook.

Settling into a comfortable armchair looking out on the early summer sunny evening, which would shortly be turning to dusk, Michael held the glass of chardonnay to his lips, took a sip to clear his throat, then spoke in a clear prepared manner.

"You will remember at our meeting a week or so ago to discuss the Peace Agreement I indicated to you all that the result of the vote would mean changes to our strategy." The couple opposite nodded in agreement. "And the need to include targeting of economic projects that would affect the British Government's income."

"There are not many areas that can bring widespread devastation to an economy. We could attack and render useless a power station, but only attacking a nuclear plant would give us the attention we desire. It would have disastrous consequences for large sections of the community and would result in thousands of deaths of innocent people if it all went wrong. Obviously attacks on oil rigs are impractical although we may consider hitting an oil pipeline in future, or one of the refineries, which would bring to a halt, huge parts of the business community. Manufacturing would be interrupted; workers laid off and ultimately tax revenues diminished thus affecting the British Balance of Payments ratios. But that's not what I have in mind at present.'

Getting up from his chair Michael crossed the room and opened up his cocktail cabinet, reached in and brought out a bottle of Dewar's White Label, turned round to face his colleagues and standing before them explained, "No this is what I have in mind" he said holding the bottle aloft. "The whisky industry in the UK is worth, according to last year's exchequer figures over £2bn to the British economy. It accounts for a quarter of the exchequer's revenue from food and drink and has the further benefit that, if large parts of the whisky stocks were blown up, they cannot be replaced overnight as spirit has to lie at least three years to qualify as Scotch Whisky."

The figures brought a sparkle to Colm Murphy's eyes, "Very clever Michael. So, the Brits would have their income reduced and not be able to make up the shortfall without raising taxes, which would make Blair's government even more unpopular. So how do you make this happen"'

Michael Caldwell reached for a folder, opened it and commenced reading from a prepared script that he had learned off by heart, "Whisky production is very fragmented due to each local community having their own unique single malt. There are close to one hundred malt distilleries but only half a dozen grain distilleries. The grain distilleries produce the bulk whisky that is blended with malts to produce the popular brands. It was an Irishman, Aeneus Coffey, a custom's officer from Dublin who became Inspector General for Customs in Ireland, who invented the Coffey Still in 1830 which expanded whisky production dramatically and made this possible."

Mhairi raised her glass and smiled "A toast to Irish ingenuity - sorry Michael I interrupted you, please carry on."

Her leader smiled "There's nothing we Irish like better than a claim to have made alcohol available more efficiently. However, getting back to the drawing board it is the volume brands that require the large whisky stocks and in recent years there has been a policy of bonding large stocks of spirit near bottling halls that are, for fire purposes, well away from high density population centres. This is where I think we can upset the status quo if we can penetrate the whisky stocks and place an explosive device inside the bonds."

Colm Murphy felt compelled to speak up, "Michael, this carries a high tariff risk to human life and goes entirely against what you said last week about not wanting to be involved in large-scale killings. There are probably hundreds of workers involved between the bottling plants and the bonds so I am not happy to go along with this."

"Calm yourself, Colm, remember the purpose of the exercise is to upset the British coffers. Before anything went off, the usual warnings given regarding a largescale bomb would be issued to British security, in time for them to evacuate the area, but not find our explosives. The device could be on a timer and the threat to the Brits is; if they do not comply with the messages we have conveyed through the media to them, they will be responsible for the consequences. The alternative is to negotiate a ransom from Downing Street but this is unlikely to happen as they have long had a policy since the Thatcher days of non-negotiation with terrorists."

Mhairi McClure asked, "So what is the plan and where do I come into it"

"A timely interjection Mhairi. I was just coming to you and it ties in nicely" Caldwell said, pointing to the papers for the Birmingham Conference, "During our trip to

69

Aston University, when delegates from all over the UK descend on Birmingham, I would like you to familiarise yourself, or be familiar with, however you want to put it with Allan Phair, a professor of chemistry from Edinburgh University who is an expert on the whisky industry. Allan gets a retainer from the Scotch Whisky Association and apart from his academic input into the whisky trade, also sits on their security committee. He will be able to enlighten you on what level of security they have in place and we can then decide how it can be breached."

From behind his papers Michael produced a photograph and handed it to Mhairi "Here's your man."

Mhairi accepted the photograph, looked at the image of a handsome man "He is very attractive and in my age bracket."

"He's married to Hilary who is also an academic but they are well known for leading a very free life and both have had extra marital liaisons in the past. He treats the USC as a boy's week so I'm sure you will be able to get an audience with him no bother."

"I'm sure I will" replied Mhairi, placing Allan Phair's photo in her briefcase.

"Where are we staying during the USC?" enquired Colm.

"I was going to book into the Hyatt, but it is too far from the NEC where the majority of the seminars are being held, so I have settled for De Vere at Forest of Arden. I've been there before, it is comfortable, has a good sports facility and a great golf course which will be well used that week. By the way Mhairi, your target Allan

Phair, as expected from most Scots, is an accomplished golfer who is a member of Aberlady Links, an exclusive golf club in East Lothian, a male bastion establishment devoid of members of the fairer sex."

"No wonder he likes a bit on the side - oh, I can't believe that I referred to myself as that! Only joking", she added noticing the frown on the other two's faces.

Seeing the funny side Michael Caldwell stood up, smiled, and bringing their meeting to a close announced "Dinner will now be served".

●　　●　　●　　●　　●

After the short journey across the Irish Sea, Flight EZY 456 landed at Birmingham Airport with a bump that woke some of the passengers from their early morning slumbers and spilt the last few drops of Colm Murphy's coffee.

"Damn it", he growled, "That's the first of my two silk ties ruined before we are even off the plane!"

No sympathy was shown by either Michael or Mhairi although the latter suggested, "That one is no loss - it doesn't go with your present outfit nor unfortunately any other one I have seen you in before. Do us all a favour and donate it to the first charity shop we see!"

After entering into the terminal, the trio made their way to the Baggage Hall where they waited for their luggage for what seemed an age. This was not altogether unexpected as Birmingham Airport officials had seen what the IRA had done to Birmingham City Centre in the 1970s. They did not want to relax their security procedures for fear of falling foul to a bomb that would devastate the airport but more importantly have untold serious complications for the airport's future ability to attract new business to Birmingham. There was a large Irish community in the city who were capable of safely igniting explosives by giving prior warnings to the local media. The lull in proceedings gave the Irish contingent time to observe the other passengers lining up at the other baggage carousels and Michael paid particular attention to the one provided for arrivals from Edinburgh.

"Allan!" shouted Michael in a loud voice that startled his companions, "How are you doing?"

The tall figure of Allan Phair turned round to see who was addressing him, "Michael Caldwell! Well now I know the Irish are here we are going to have a bit of a hoolie tonight, after listening to conference all day." Allan approached Michael with a firm handshake that gave Michael a chance to introduce his colleagues.

"Allan, I don't think you will have met my team Professor Colm Murphy who heads up our Financial Studies Chair and Mhairi McClure our expert in the field of computer studies."

"Pleased to make your acquaintance Colm" said Allan as he shook hands and turning to Mhairi went a stage further with a handshake and two continental kisses on the cheek, "and it's lovely to start the day in the company of such an attractive lady."

Mhairi did not respond as quickly as Michael who interjected, "And we're supposed to be the ones with the blarney." Already knowing the answer Michael continued "Where are you staying during the conference?"

"Forrest of Arden" confirmed Allan.

"Great, so are we. So, we'll probably see you in the bar after dinner for a nightcap or three." arranged Michael. "Sounds good to me" replied the Scotsman with a wide smile before returning back to his own luggage conveyor.

After getting their luggage the Antrim three moved off in the direction of the taxi rank. Mhairi opened the conversation "Well he's everything I expected tall, blond, handsome and more than capable of sweeping some defenceless computer studies professor off her feet and into his bed!"

Her companions smiled before Colm passed some words of advice, "Mhairi, you're supposed to be playing hard to get and extracting information from him, don't let the side down by smothering him in a passionate seduction after a couple of drinks and giving him the opportunity to seek out pastures new."

"Point taken Colm" replied Mhairi thinking of how difficult it will be not to rip the clothes off Allan Phair over the next few days.

After the short four-mile taxi ride the trio soon found themselves in the reception of Forrest of Arden Country Club in all its five-star glory, set in two hundred acres of woodland which included a championship golf course.

Colm attracted the beautiful Asian receptionist's attention before starting his opening gambit," We have three rooms booked under Antrim University in the name of Caldwell, McClure and Murphy for two nights. We are attending the USC conference so they may be booked under that banner."

The receptionist typed quickly into her computer before responding, "Ah yes here we are Miss McClure is in Room 216, Mr Caldwell 147 and you Mr Murphy are in 323. The organisers asked that we spread the delegates throughout the hotel in order to encourage intercommunication. Breakfast is available from 6.30a.m.; the spa is open from 7.00a.m. Until 10.00p.m. There is a choice of restaurants where dinner is served from 6.30p.m. last orders being taken at 9.30p.m. The bars all stay open until 1.00a.m., for those of you who want to let your hair down there is a discotheque in the basement that finishes at 2.00a.m. Anyone requiring any further refreshments will be able to obtain them from the night porter."

"Thank goodness for that' smiled Michael Caldwell, "if past conferences are to go by drink will be consumed well into the small hours."

The receptionist continued, "Here are your keys, and we hope you have a pleasant stay. My name is Jazi and if there is anything you want please call me."

"Thank you." the visitors replied in unison before Michael instructed "Right it's only 10.30. Let's get settled into the rooms and meet back here at 11.15. We have to be across at the NEC for 1.00 so it will give us a chance to have a chat before heading off."

The other two nodded and headed for the lifts.

Forty-five minutes later Mhairi joined Michael and Colm at a quiet table in the corner of the Oaks Bar.

"Being here first I ordered coffee and biscuits" announced Colm, "as we will have to leave here in just over the hour."

"Good" said Michael, "you are both aware of what we require for the university so let's concentrate on Allan Phair. He is joining us for drinks after our meal in the Oaks Restaurant. I see you have made a big impression on him Mhairi, so you should be able to keep his full attention tonight. How you go about getting his attention - and keeping it for several hours- is your affair. What we want to know is how the larger distilleries bond their produce? Where stock is kept? What security measures are taken to ensure it is safe from terrorist attack? Allan sits in on all the Scotch Whisky Association Security Council meetings so his information should be state of the art."

Mhairi shuffled nervously in her seat, "I am confident that I will be able to seduce Allan Phair, but I don't want my technique scrutinised by you two, so can I ask you to call it a night at midnight and leave the fun and games to me."

Colm smiled, "Is that when you turn into a raving nympho, Mhairi. Oh, to be a fly on the wall!"

Mhairi responded, "You'd be swatted away instantly or suffocated in the vibrating blankets." she joked.

Michael interjected and getting to his feet counselled,

"Too much information Mhairi, time for us to get to the NEC. I'm going to check out reception for any messages. Give me your keys and I'll hand them in."

Mhairi handed over the key that Michael then placed in a plastic box and finally into a padded envelope as he made his way to the front desk. The receptionist smiled and Michael asked if she would keep the package for a 'Mr. Malcolm' who would collect it within the hour. True to form Mr. Malcolm picked up the package twenty minutes after the party had left for the NEC and made his way to Room 216 where he put the 'do not disturb' sign on the door while he installed surveillance equipment. After he had finished he took a cast of the key to get a replica made for his return visit the next day.

The USC started with an opening speech from Dr. Jonathon Haggan welcoming the six hundred delegates before going on to outline the importance of the role universities played in developing the future of the United Kingdom. Guiding the best brains in the country to seek careers that would keep Great Britain at the forefront of the developing world at present under threat from the merging nations in Asia and in the long-term, the African Continent. Feed-back and exchange of ideas was what the conference was all about. He then instructed the delegates to disperse into their pre-arranged groups and discuss their allocated topic.

 Mhairi's group contained an engineering professor from Bristol University, Jim Robertson, an economics guru from the LSE, Professor Stanley Bing, Legal expert, Nigel Prince, from Cambridge and Allan Phair. Their discussion topic was 'How do we transport inventions from the laboratory to the marketplace without passing control or leaking any secrets to overseas competitors.'

A lively discussion prevailed with all parties contributing their tuppence worth using their own area of expertise and explaining how they saw the boffins in the educational establishments throughout the land could bring benefit to the UK economy of the future. Mhairi saw an opportunity to open her dialogue with Allan Phair.

"Dr Phair..."

"Allan please" interrupted the Scotsman

"Allan" continued Mhairi, "Did I not read somewhere that you are a consultant to the Scotch whisky industry? So, in regard to our topic for discussion, 'about containing confidentiality' is there anything in your experience we can recommend to minimise intelligence being passed on illegally? I would imagine your clients must have some very sophisticated systems in place."

Allan Phair replied, "Colleagues, the Scotch Whisky industry has long had to fight off threats from overseas competitors engaged in passing off fake whisky supplies. We take these actions very seriously and have campaigned successfully to protect our industry by stating that Scotch Whisky must be blended and bottled in Scotland. More recently Harris Tweed has also protected their material by stating that it must have a kite-mark to say it has been spun in Harris. I must admit I wish the textile industry had protected itself in the same way regarding tartan as I cringe when I see tourists in the centre of Edinburgh being sold kilts that are just cheap crap, produced in some Far -East sweatshop."

"Returning to the whisky trade our members are extremely protective regarding the content of their particular blended brand of whisky. This of course doesn't apply to single malt whiskies which are identified by the area in Scotland from where they distilled and the local water that goes into their production."

Mhairi pressed on, "And do you feel comfortable that your product is safe from a physical standpoint bearing in mind that your larger bonds contain millions of gallons of raw spirit sitting around waiting to be turned into whisky?"

Allan Phair replied, "Well it is fair to say that distilleries all over Scotland apply the strictest of protocol to ensure that there are no breaches in security. It is a good point you have raised and one that I would be happy to discuss further with anyone who is interested. I think we should press on as conference will want a precis of our thoughts on how we can assist the boffins get new markets."

The panel nodded and spent the remaining time gathering their thoughts before appointing Professor Bing as their spokesman to address the conference should their group be selected to do so. Afterwards they broke up to return to in the main assembly hall. As they approached the door of the main discussion theatre Allan Phair touched Mhairi on the arm, "Thanks for your interest in the whisky trade, if you want we could meet up after dinner to enhance on our conversation?"

Mhairi was delighted to have snared her prey so quickly and blurted out, "It's a date Allan'" then realising what she had said followed up, "I'm doing a study into how computerisation can assist the drinks trade - as there could be a market for increasing Irish Whiskey sales in the future. I'll see you in the bar at ten o'clock tonight."

Arriving back at Forrest of Arden Mhairi went straight to her room where she phoned Michael and Colm inviting them to meet up in her room. Michael arrived first and prior to sitting on Mhairi's bed, headed for the mini-bar and helped himself to a miniature of whisky which he poured into one of the tumblers in the bathroom before adding tap water. A knock on the door heralded Colm's entrance and seeing Michael with a glass of Scotch he opened the mini-bar and took out a can of coke. Mhairi had already made herself a coffee.

"Well, now you have both made yourself at home I have some good news. I was in a discussion group with Allan."

'Oh, it's Allan now' mocked Colm.

"If you must know he insisted on us being on first name term"' returned Mhairi "Anyhow I was able to engage him in conversation about the whisky trade. He has invited me to meet him tonight after dinner in the bar to further our discussions over an après dinner drink. What do you think about that?"

Michael was sporting a broad grin as he responded, "Excellent Mhairi, you're quick off the mark and hopefully your 'discussions' will bear fruit. I haven't disclosed the whisky plant I have targeted to either of you and don't intend to yet. However, there are four possible targets on this list' he added reaching into his pocket and passing a note of paper to each of them, "And I would you like to obtain as much information on them as you can. Who sends them casks for filling? Where do they come from? Who supplies the transport and once they are filled how are they transported to the bond? Finally, where are the biggest bonds that are NOT in populated areas?"

Mhairi put down the pen she had used to record Michael's questions. "Can we meet for dinner at 7.30 so that we can make sure that we are in the bar in plenty of time? Allan is due in, as I say, at 10.00 so I would ask you two to be sociable and stay for a couple of drinks before making an excuse that you have some financial reports to scrutinise in connection with Colm's presentation tomorrow. That will leave the way clear for me to concentrate on the randy Scotsman."

Colm asked, "Have you decided on your game plan yet?"

Mhairi smiled back, "Naturally, I'm quite good at undercover work."

Her colleagues silence emphasised their embarrassment before Michael sheepishly muttered "See you downstairs
for dinner."

Chapter 12

Mhairi's entrance into the Oaks restaurant caused occupants to turn heads and ogle at her outfit. She was wearing a black satin halter-necked cat suit with a plunging neckline pulled tight by a bow behind her neck. It certainly showed off her figure, leaving nothing to the imagination. The outfit was set off by a jewelled choker and finished with a pair of black stiletto high heels. Her blond shoulder length hair, was combed back over her ears into a French roll and she had applied just the right amount of make-up. On her approach to the table both Michael and Colm rose to their feet as if to let the rest of the diners know that she was their date.

Colm couldn't contain himself, "Well Miss McClure, I can see that you're ready for the disco and if you don't rope your target in that outfit the man's celibate!"

Michael was more reserved in his appreciation of his colleague, "Mhairi you look absolutely amazing, good enough to almost affect my appetite- but not quite, so let's examine the menu."

The food lived up to their expectations and they concluded by asking the waiter to serve them their coffee and liqueurs in the bar. It was 9.35 when they settled down in their armchairs and the coffee arrived five minutes later. Michael gathered his brandy in his palm, swirling the glass before raising it and making a toast "Here's to a successful night."

Mhairi smiled, "I'll second that."

Allan Phair arrived right on time at the Antrim table and sat down - at the same time attracting the waitress to come and take a drinks order before remarking, "Well that was a lovely meal and substantial enough to allow me a few drinks to wash it down."

Michael responded, "Unfortunately Colm and I will have to curtail ourselves to a couple of drinks as we have work to do, but Mhairi here is keen to find out more about the whisky trade for a project she is addressing. So, she'll keep you busy on our behalf."

Allan broke out into a smile, "Well no disrespect gentlemen, but I will be the envy of all the men in the hotel to be entertaining such an attractive lady and may I say Mhairi you look stunning this evening."

Mhairi felt her face going red with all the attention she was receiving but braved it out by replying "It's not often that a girl goes to all the bother to get ready for the disco only to find her two partners are abandoning her."

"Don't worry Mhairi," mused Michael, "Dr Phair will be more than able to make up for us two with him coming from Scotland where they specialise in country dancing or 'jiggin' as they refer to it. Is that not so Allan?"

Playing along with the theme Allan responded, "Of course I'm out 'reelin' every night back home - dressed in my kilt - but my movements will be restricted this evening as normally we true Scots take to the dancefloor in our kilts with nothing underneath!"

Everyone laughed and Mhairi smiled before remarking, "Well, now it really is a pity that we didn't give you more warning about the disco."

The conversation continued in a light mood for another hour until Michael caught Colm's attention and getting up out of his chair announced, "Okay Colm come on some of us have work to do - we'll leave you two to strut the disco floor."

After they had left the room Allan turned to Mhairi, "I thought they'd never leave. Now Miss McClure tell me all about yourself. Where did you go to Uni and how did you end up in academia?"

Mhairi looked longingly into his pale blue eyes before answering, "Before I expose my CV to you can I continue our earlier conversation about the problems of trying to expand the Irish Whisky industry. From a novice's point of view, I'm surprised we have not done so earlier as we are geographically so close to Scotland. Even somewhere like Islay, which is only twenty-five miles from the Irish coast has six distilleries."

"Good point" Allan agreed, "There are slight chemical differences in the water but I think it is worth pursuing. Actually, a hundred years ago Irish Whiskey was produced at over thirty distilleries. This has declined and today there are only a handful remaining. Security could be a problem for you as whiskey is a very flammable product when it comes off the still at one hundred and twenty proof although this diminishes once evaporation occurs bringing it down to eighty over. Nevertheless, if you will permit me to say so there are factions in Northern Ireland who like to create publicity by the blowing up of industrial installations?"

"So how can we guard against this sort of thing happening? Scottish distilleries must have good security in place." Mhairi inquired.

Allan continued," Yes Customs & Excise play a large part in making sure consignments of spirit move around the country in Crown Locked Vehicles or CLVs as they are known. These lorries are sealed by a Customs Watcher, or guard you would call him, at the distillery where the barrels on board have been filled and examined by the receiving customs officer at the bond, where the barrels will be stored a minimum of three years to mature. Thereafter they are consigned to a Bottling Hall to be blended and bottled into what we have on the shelves over there." Allan pointed at the well-stocked bar to their left. "Nowadays the larger whisky companies tend to have their bonds close by their bottling plants to save on transportation costs. Having everything together makes it easier for them to 'badge market their product line."

"Do you find there is a lot of petty stealing goes on with the workforce?"

"Yes, there is always someone trying to beat the system, generally new employees but we do spot searches usually when shifts are ending and anyone caught with bottles are immediately sacked."

"Quite right too", Mhairi declared "I suppose there is no point in searching them on the way in unless you want to see what they are having for lunch."

"Correct" observed Allan, whom Mhairi sensed was showing signs of boredom, "and anyway there are excellent canteen facilities. Now let me here about your CV."

"I was at Oxford before doing a Masters in computer studies at Harvard."

"Harvard" Allan interrupted, "now that must have been interesting - did you adjust to the American way of life?"

"Oh yes, although they do have a different way of living! All fast food and an incredible ignorance of geography as they don't teach their school kids anything about the world out with mainland USA!"

"And as for their taste in sports..." Allan added, "Ice hockey, basketball and playing American football wearing helmets and heavy padding in what looks like legalised assault and battery."

"I actually enjoyed American football and wished there had been a lady's team." murmured Mhairi.

"Really" Allan replied with raised eyebrows, "So where in the team would you fit in?"

Mhairi hesitated, cocking her head before letting her tongue lick her upper lip and looking into her victim's eyes she replied "Oh I'm a wide receiver."

After a moment of silence Mhairi suggested, "Is it not about time we tried the disco?"

Offering her his hand Allan gestured in the direction of the music, "As they say in the Nike advert 'Let's do it."

When they entered the disco, it was in full fling with a great cross-section of British academia expending brawn power rather than brain power as they gyrated to Chuck Berry's sixties classic 'No Particular Place to Go'. Allan and Mhairi tried to continue their conversation but could not make themselves heard. After the third ear, shattering number Allan signalled it was time to head back to the bar. On reaching an oasis of silence Mhairi turned to Allan, "Well that's a relief to be out of there."

"You can say that again" responded Allan, taking Mhairi in his arms, "So what can we do for an encore?"

Mhairi felt her body reacting to his hold, "The bars probably quietened down now but we could have a nightcap upstairs instead." she suggested. "Best offer I've had for a while. Let's get in the lift."

By the time the lift reached the second floor the couple had entered into heavy petting with Allan exploring Mhairi's body and she responding by using her tongue to survey his mouth. After a brief search, the key to room 216 burst open the door and more serious foreplay began with Allan throwing off his jacket before grasping Mhairi and untying the bow of her cat-suit making it fall to her ankles to reveal her very provocative underwear. She tearing away at his shirt, before placing her hand on the swelling in his trouser, then unzipping his fly and pulling both his trousers and underpants off to reveal his considerable manhood. Allan undid her bra kissing her breasts and then ran his hand in between her legs at which point Mhairi put a cautioning hand over his, "Sorry Allan, wrong time of the month," she lied having previously inserted a tampon coated with tomato sauce. She then started nibbling down his body until she held his manhood in her hand, "I did say I was a wide receiver." as she opened her mouth wide to finish off the seduction in style.

At that point Allan moved quickly "Come on, I'm not put off by a little mess." and before she could move back up the bed he was inside her removing the tampon, "What's this? Smells like ketchup to me –you lying bitch! You're going to get it now."

The smiling professor now turned into a sex fiend as he overwhelmed Mhairi and forced himself on her, placing his free hand on her neck and warning her not to scream. Mhairi was frightened and succumbed to what she had been wanting to happen all night but the sudden change in Allan's behaviour disgusted her.

After several minutes which seemed a lifetime to Mhairi, a few grunts indicated to her that he had satisfied himself. He rolled over and lay panting beside her.

Mhairi felt an urge to kill him but vowed that she would leave her revenge for now.

Allan dressed quickly and was about to leave the room when he turned back to look at the crumpled figure in the bed with her head buried in the sheets, "Sorry about that, but I don't like to be made a fool of."

Chapter 14

Next morning Colm and Michael waited anxiously at the breakfast table but Mhairi didn't appear. "It must have been a good night and our little Mata Hari is going for a heavy breakfast if you know what I mean." Colm mused.

"I don't think so Colm, Professor Phair has just entered the dining room."

Michael beckoned him over, "Morning Allan, did you manage to help Mhairi with her whisky project?"

"Yes, I gave a full account of myself." he replied, "well I better be off, three sessions to attend, then I'm having a round of golf later this afternoon before dinner."

"A full day! You've certainly worked up some energy overnight" Colm joked.

"Well that's what happens when you fraternise with the Irish." replied the Scotsman before turning and heading for the foyer.

Twenty minutes passed and still no sign of Mhairi. Michael was becoming concerned and made his way up to Room 216, where his first knock on the door did not get a response. He knocked louder and said, "Mhairi, its Michael."

He heard the door lock unbolt and Mhairi gingerly opened the door to expose only her head. "Morning Michael, come in."

"Morning. How are you today? We were getting concerned when you didn't appear. Did everything go okay with Allan Phair last night?"

Looking away Mhairi muttered, "Yes fine. He gave me a breakdown of the security procedures which I think we can use."

Michael was used to judging body language and he knew something was not right. "What's wrong? You look as though you haven't slept a wink - how can I say this - did you have an overactive evening?"

Mhairi turned to address her leader, "Well, you could say I took one for the team but..." she felt her eyes welling up and her body trembling.

Michael stepped forward and placed a fatherly arm on her shoulder and leading her to a seat on the unmade bed said, "Come on, sit down and tell me all about it."

Mhairi swallowed hard before managing to blurt out "He, he raped me when I told him that I did not want to have sex with him as it was the wrong time of the month. That did not deter him from forcing himself upon me. He held me down and left his mark on me." Opening the top three buttons of her silk blouse and pulling down the front of her bra she revealed the marks that her assailant had imprinted on her flesh.

Michael Caldwell was shell-shocked by what he had seen and could not refrain from displaying his anger, "What a bastard! I have known him for years and it is well known that he dabbles in affairs of the flesh but I never suspected for a minute that he would resort to this kind

89

of behaviour. Words fail me and I do not know how I can apologise for what has happened."

Mhairi had calmed down a little and was able to reply, "Michael, you were not to know. After he had his way I could genuinely have killed him. There is little point in reporting this to the police as a defence lawyer would have a field day not to mention the tabloids who would ruin my career and bring attention to our cause which we can do without."

"I'm sorry Mhairi. I will seek revenge but right now my anger prevents me from deciding at what level. Once I have calmed down I will decide my course of action. Look, you are in no fit state to attend the conference. I'll tell Colm that you have a stomach upset and we will see you when we get back from the NEC."

"Thanks Michael, I appreciate it if you do not make Colm any the wiser at this stage. I don't want any unruly scenes downstairs in the bar once he has had a few drinks."

"Okay, I better be off. Colm will be waiting in the foyer"' Michael concluded before closing the door quietly behind him. Colm accepted Michael's explanation for Mhairi's absence and they set off for the NEC.

Ten hours later, having had a full day listening to academics making promises to secure the future of the United Kingdom through enhanced education and research programmes, Michael headed straight for the Zest bar. He ordered a large Talisker whisky with ice and water which he left untouched until he had downed a half pint of John Smith's ale to quench his initial thirst. Picking up his glass and a paper off the bar, he retired to a nearby armchair to catch up with the latest world news and let his mind wander as to what action he was going to take in regard to the previous evening's events in Room 216. His reading was interrupted by a noisy foursome entering the bar. Allan Phair obviously fresh from the golf course was one of them.

Leaning on the bar, a red-faced balding fifty-year-old turned to the other three, "Gentlemen allow me to buy the drinks to celebrate our victory with Allan's excellent birdie three at the eighteenth. What's your pleasure?" The other three golfers made their choice then spent the next ten minutes going over the events of the last three hours. Once they exhausted the match they discussed golf in general before Cyril Thomas, a small white haired tubby professor from Cardiff, changed the subject slightly.

"Allan, I understand you are a member of an all-male club near Edinburgh which is renowned for not allowing women to play on the course. Is that true?"

"It sure is. One of my friends told me that he, and his guests, witnessed the secretary taking a phone call from someone based in San Diego which went as follows:

'You're phoning from where?

San Diego - what time is it there?

Two a.m. Good God!

Yes, you can play here - your wife?

No, she can't play here.

The caller continued to persist until our old secretary inflicted his coup de grace. "Sir you don't seem to understand, women are inconsequential here!"

His remarks were met with a hail of laughter before Cyril gathered himself, "Christ can you imagine the lawsuits if he had said that in the States."

Allan looked at the others before continuing with a smile "I would fall in with the sec's opinion if it weren't for the fact that I need a good woman on a regular basis and I do not curtail my needs to the family home."

"Yes, we saw you in action last night with that Irish girl - a very attractive lady I might add. Did she fit your bill?" asked Bob Ritchie from Inverness.

Allan Phair smiled mischievously, "You might think so, but I couldn't possibly comment." Leaving his audience to let their imaginations run riot he added, "Time to go and shower before dinner."

"Smug bastard" thought Michael Caldwell whose reaction was to let Allan Phair go before leaving the bar and returning to his room to decide on his strategy. Before long he would be picking up the phone to call Seamus Carr and 'PK.'

When the phone rang Seamus Carr had just bitten into his latest McDonalds purchase and the tone made him grab his drink to wash down the contents of his mouth before pressing the answer key on his mobile. "Hello," he croaked.

"Seamus is that you?" enquired Michael Caldwell.

"Yes, you have caught me having a carry out."

"Time you got yourself a woman. Just giving you a ring to see how your man got on with the survey last night."

"He picked up the key you left for Room 216 and placed the camera strategically to get the widest view of the area. However, he has not been able to recover it as the occupant has not left the room today but he will go back when the room is vacated in the morning."

Michael interrupted Carr, "How long does he need to recover the camera?" "Oh, only a couple of minutes."

"Right Seamus, put him on standby. I'll invite the occupant to dinner and will text you to say when he can enter Room 216." Michael added, "Remember Seamus, under no circumstances must your man look at the content of the film - if he values his life." Michael stated threateningly.

Michael placed the phone on its cradle then picked it up again and dialled through to Mhairi's room where it was answered after three rings, "Mhairi McClure speaking,"

"Hello Mhairi," replied Michael, "I have just got back from the Conference - you didn't miss much by the way. I wanted to know if you are going to join us for dinner this evening."

There was a silence for a few seconds before Mhairi said, "Yes, that would be nice. I have been in my room all day so could we meet in the foyer and have a stroll round the grounds prior to eating."

"Good idea Mhairi, I could do with the exercise, is it okay if I invite Colm?"

"Yes, but not a word about last night unless I tell you."

"Understood, meet you in the foyer at seven o'clock" Michael replied and put down the phone, only to immediately picked it up again.

"Seamus, Michael again. Tell your man to be in the foyer just before seven o'clock to see me meeting the lady in Room 216. We are going to have a walk in the garden and that should give him sufficient time to disconnect the camera, remove the film and leave it in an envelope at reception for me to collect later."

"I'll give him the message. You'll know him when you see him, and he's a wee fella with a crew-cut and wears thick horn-rimmed glasses. Bye for now."

Michael was intrigued to see the electronics expert who had bugged Mhairi's room to obtain the vital piece of evidence he needed before deciding on Professor Phair's fate. At 6.55p.m. Michael passed through reception into the Zest Bar where the young man Seamus Carr had described was sitting on a stool dressed casually in sports gear. Reading a paper and guarding his sports bag that contained his electronic tools he looked like the most unlikely terrorist but Michael had scrutinised his CV before allowing him to complete his mission and it made interesting reading. After taking his degree in electrical engineering 'Mr Malcolm' had through friends at college volunteered his services to the IRA cause and had planted a number of explosive devices that had resulted in mayhem and considerable loss of life. He enjoyed his work and would be useful to Michael for what he had in store for the British Government.

"Evening Michael. We met in the lift," explained Colm, who was wearing an open-necked check shirt and brush cotton fawn slacks. Standing next to him Mhairi had toned down her outfit from the previous evening to grey slacks, a white blouse that she covered with a dark brown round neck lambswool sweater.

"I was just telling Mhairi how pleased I was to see her back on her feet and that she will have to attend the lectures tomorrow so that I can have a day off."

A smile came over Mhairi's face, "Well Colm, you picked the wrong day as we finish at noon and we're on the 3.30p.m. back to Belfast."

"Ah, Mhairi you are always a step ahead of me, so you are"

"Come on you two" called Michael striding towards the gardens, "time for a quick walk round the estate before dinner."

The gardens were beautifully kept and overlooked the golf course where the last players were racing dusk to complete their rounds. As they walked in silence all that could be heard was the crunching of the white granite chips below their feet. Michael disliked the eeriness and ended it by asking, "Have you found the conference useful or do you think it is time that academia stopped these jollies and communicated electronically in the future"'

Colm chose to answer the question, "Economically it would make sense to correspond electronically but of course you lose the personal touch - there is no substitute for pressing the flesh."

"Most unfortunate terminology." thought Michael, glancing sideways at Mhairi but she was unfazed or had not connected his words with the previous evening's activities.

"As a computer science professional" contributed Mhairi, "I would hope to see great strides in technology in the near future which will result in an increase in conferencing electronically so that we can sit in our offices in Antrim and debate the topics of the day."

"But you would miss any nocturnal liaisons with Professor Phair" Colm retorted.

"Oh God, Colm, I wondered when you would get on to that subject. Since you're asking, I might as well tell you that our little plan worked fairly well and I have gathered the information we required. However, I can tell you that I have no plans to see Allan Phair again this evening."

"Well put." thought Michael before continuing, "Colm, I think we should drop that subject for present as Mhairi has had an uncomfortable day with her upset stomach and she needs to make the most of this lovely fresh air before we go for something to eat. I thought we should try the Zest Restaurant this evening as it is less formal both sartorially and in the culinary delights it serves up."

Colm turned and gave his apology: "Sorry Mhairi, I wasn't trying to pry and I won't raise the subject again"

"Accepted Colm, now let's get back into the hotel, I don't like the look of these gathering clouds."

The meal passed off without further reference to Allan Phair. They concentrated instead on discussing the policy at Antrim College and of how improvements could be instigated into the tutorial programmes. Another lengthy discussion led them thinking on how they could establish greater co-operation with academic establishments in Northern Ireland. Apart from the academic benefits this would camouflage their extra curriculum activities but at the same time make them party to snippets of gossip regarding Ulster Defence Force activities.

The three academics retired to the bar for a night-cap and having settled into a quiet corner their tranquillity was interrupted by the same golfing foursome that Michael had encountered earlier. Michael found himself agitated by the thought that Allan Phair looked hell bent on another night of laddish behaviour and was concerned how Mhairi would react to it. One of the four Peter Anderton, an economist from Bristol University approached the bar and acknowledged the Irish presence before asking in an inebriated voice, "Evening Miss McClure. Shall we be seeing you later on the dance floor strutting your stuff again tonight?"

Mhairi stared at Phillips before answering, "No Peter, I'm not up to revelling two nights in a row."

"That's not the impression Allan gave us" replied Peter in a loud voice, turning to his three colleagues, "Was it Phairy, old boy."

Colm moved quickly off his seat in the direction of the man from Bristol with only one thought in mind, to knock his head off. He was beaten to the punch by Allan

97

Phair who grabbed him by the collar and marched him out the bar shouting, "You're out of order Peter, time you went to bed."

Five minutes later Allan returned to the bar, came right up to Mhairi's table and opening his arms in forgiveness mode uttered, "Mhairi, I would like to apologise for my friend's remarks. They were totally uncalled for."

Mhairi felt her cheeks go red at being made the centre of attention but still managed to reply, "Accepted Allan, but I am disappointed that the memory of last night's activities have been spoiled by the thought that they may have been shared by other attendees at the conference." At this point she rose to leave the room but Allan stood in her way.

"Mhairi I am really sorry."

"Get out of my way before I call security."

Colm intervened, "That won't be necessary. I'll deck him right now."

Michael could see what was about to happen and quickly stood between the two men, "Gentlemen, can I remind you of your positions and how the gutter press would report a fracas between two leading academics. Mhairi, you go on your way, Allan you sit down with me for moment and Colm, you go and get some cool air to calm you down."

Mhairi and Colm obeyed their superior and went on their respected ways. Michael turned to Allan Phair and looked him in the eye before saying, "I don't know what gets into you Allan. How you conduct your life is your affair and is a matter for your conscience but when it involves a member of my staff I take a very close interest." Looking over his shoulder to make sure nobody was within earshot he continued, "Living in the Provence brings me into contact with some very unsavoury groups, who are due me some favours. So, if I were you I would not utter another word about last night or you could be entering the one-armed golfers' championship. Am I making myself clear?"

Allan could not believe what he had just heard and was about to protest when he surveyed the stern look on Caldwell's face and the mad look in his eyes as he repeated, "Am I making myself clear Allan?"

Chapter 15

Life was soon back to normal in Antrim. After a couple of days spent catching up on correspondence and briefs from his staff Michael promised himself a night in with his dog and the tape that 'Mr Malcolm' had left for him at the Forrest of Arden reception.

Settling down in his armchair with a large whisky and ice he started the tape. Twenty minutes later he wiped away the tear that was running down his cheek brought on by the guilt of having subjected Mhairi to such a vicious assault from Allan Phair.

Some aspects of his double life didn't worry Michael Caldwell but the contents of the tape made him think how low his moral standards had sunk. What would his wife, or his son, an innocent victim caught in the path of an army patrol, think of the changes that Michael had introduced into his lifestyle, in an effort to overcome the personal grief he suffered since the loss of his son.

For the next couple of hours, over a considerable consumption of alcohol, he argued with himself on how he should deal with Allan Phair. Several outcomes haunted his mind but whatever he decided would not be carried out by him personally. There was only one thing for it. Lifting the phone, he dialled a special number for one of his close contacts and waited while it rang ten times before a voice answered. "Pat Kearney."

"PK, it's Michael, how are you doing?"

"Just fine, I've been working hard hear keeping things tickety-boo while you were away last week in Birmingham living it up."

"All necessary hard work PK. Look, the reason for my call is that I want to get your advice on a matter that needs your expertise. Could you come round to the house on Thursday night about eight o'clock?"

"Yes, that should be okay Michael - oh wait a minute, I've got to pick up my grandson from boxing at seventhirty so will eight thirty be all right?" he asked.

"No problem Pat, I'm not an early bedder. See you Thursday night. Goodnight."

On Thursday evening Luke's barking announced the arrival of PK in his silver Volvo estate car and made Michael Caldwell glance at his watch which told him he was ten minutes early. He opened the front door and Luke bounded out in the direction of the new arrival barking and wagging his tail as he did so. PK quickly got out the car and met the onrushing Border collie.

"Hello Luke how are you boy?" he asked giving the dog's coat a good few pats on the back. Continuing on his way he offered his hand to Michael. "Good evening, I managed to get away a little early - my grandson won his bout inside the distance."

"He must take out his aggressive nature from his grandfather" Michael joked, "Come on in and I'll get you a drink, what would you like?"

"Just a coffee Michael. I don't want to give the B Specials any reason to get me into the police station if I don't have to."

Michael directed PK into his large kitchen where he made coffee for both of them and exchanging pleasantries before the two men took their mugs through to the lounge along with a packet of chocolate digestive biscuits. Once they had settled into the leather armchairs Michael began his address to PK.

"Thanks for coming out tonight. The reason for my call is that I have a rather awkward, some might say delicate situation, partially of my own making. It involves Mhairi. Remember I said a few weeks ago that I wanted to hurt the British Government financially and on that basis, I set out to gather information on the Scotch whisky industry. This involved using Mhairi to cross examine Allan Phair a Scottish chemistry professor who advises the Scotch whisky industry and has a reputation for having a weakness for the fair sex. What I am about to tell you PK is purely between you and me."

PK nodded his acceptance before Michael continued.

"At the academic conference, we were at in Birmingham we met up with Professor Phair and unbeknown to Mhairi I had her room bugged with a camera as I wanted evidence to blackmail Allan Phair. Unfortunately, my strategy was proved irresponsible as I did not allow for the actions of Allan as you will see from the video I am about to show you. This is not very pretty I must warn you."

Aiming the remote control at his television he pressed 'play' and the actions in Room 216 began.

As the couple commenced their activities in earnest PK gasped "Good God, who would have thought Mhairi McClure had such secret talents" but as they reached the point where Phair had forced himself on their colleague his attitude changed, "What a skunk! Nobody should condone a man for that kind of behaviour."

Five minutes later Michael switched off the film and there was a pregnant silence before he looked PK in the face, "It's very disturbing and I am determined not to let Allan Phair get away with it. As I said earlier I originally wanted to blackmail him but after his disgusting behaviour I want you to take him out. How and when is up to you."

PK sat back in his chair, and looking up to the ceiling began to assess his options: "Michael, I have taken out many opponents of our movement but I do not take my actions lightly. If I am going to end somebody's life I have to be sure they deserve it. That film is disturbing but I am a little uneasy about what I have seen as I am not sure Mhairi is as innocent as you think."

His remark caused Michael Caldwell to respond viciously, "What the hell do you mean? That Scottish bastard has inflicted himself upon one of our senior comrades and you are doubting her allegiance."

PK raised his hand in a placating manner, "Michael, can you please play the tape again and I'll explain my concerns."

Michael glowered at PK before rewinding the tape and once more pressed 'play'.

"Fast forward it until I tell you to stop." instructed PK.

Michael concurred until PK instructed "Stop! Go back a little. Perfect. Michael, now look at Mhairi's arms and how she goes from being determined to fight off Phair, to relaxing and digging her nails into his flesh, seemingly with absolute pleasure." The liaison between the couple ended and Michael went to switch off the tape but PK continued "Is there anything else on the tape, Michael?"

"I don't know, I haven't looked." said a now exasperated Caldwell.

"Fast forward it and let's see."

The tape had only been going a few seconds when the two characters began a conversation. 'Sorry Michael, we are going to have to rewind and hear what they are saying.'

In the recording they watched as Mhairi looked on, while Allan Phair picked up his crumpled trousers, then wiped her eyes, and asked, "Where are you going Allan? That was great. I love a bit of rough" and pulling back the sheets to expose her body she invited him in, "Come on get back in here."

Allan did not hesitate to get back into bed and held Mhairi in his arms as she continued looking under the covers "I see you need some recovery time so let's talk a little more about the whisky industry and how you would go about it if you were in my position."

A discussion ensued for the next twenty minutes before Mhairi started to rub Allan up, then gyrated her frame on his manhood until Allan was sapped into submission once more.

Michael stopped the tape. "Thanks for being so observant PK, I would never have thought of looking further into the tape. Mhairi has been uneconomical with the truth and maybe I have been a little hasty in my decision to kill off Allan Phair."

"Maybe so", replied PK, "But let's see the rest of the tape."

"Surely there is not more."

PK stared back at his commander, "Michael play the tape please."

The events that followed were very similar to what had gone before. Mhairi extracted even more data from Allan and then she made her move on Allan this time getting, to her knees as he entered her from behind, clearly enjoying what she referred to as 'An Irish wolfhound to finish off a good evening.'

When they finished and lay back on the bed Mhairi whispered, "Allan this has been wonderful. I would like

104

to get together again. How do you fancy another session sometime in the future?"

"Gosh, you're some woman Mhairi, and I have never been a man to turn down good sex. So yes certainly."

"Don't be upset if I give you the cold shoulder tomorrow but I don't want Michael and Colm to know that we are continuing our relationship as they might not approve as you are a married man."

"Okay, point taken. Good heavens it's five o'clock. Time I was back in my room."

"You can turn it off now Michael." PK instructed and Michael pressed the 'stop button' to bring the visuals to a close

PK sat back in his armchair before addressing his leader "Look its late and we don't want to be making any decisions tonight. Unfortunately, you are going to have to re-examine the tape again and record the dialogue so that you can compare what is said on the video, against what Mhairi McClure produces for you in her report on the Scotch whisky industry. Make sure that it is consistent with what we have been hearing and once we have all the facts then we should meet again to agree the level of punishment."

"That sounds sensible PK. We will probably have to leave this matter for a few weeks."

"Okay... then I bid you goodnight Michael'", at that he rose from his chair and headed for the door.

Six weeks passed before Michael had completed his report on Room 216. This was due partially to commitments at the university and also the delicate nature of the film meant that he could only analyse the proceedings when his wife was not in the house or had gone to bed. Patricia Caldwell was aware of her husband's connections to the republican cause but she would have disapproved profusely to his bugging of a colleague's room without their knowledge. Mhairi McClure for her part completed a dossier on her conversations with Allan Phair and there was an instant synergy in her report to what Michael had gleamed from watching the tape.

What she did not mention in the report was that in the interim there had been telephone contact between herself and her Scottish gigolo. Plans were already afoot for them to meet up in Ramsay on the Isle of Man. Information which would not go down well with Michael Caldwell if he should learn of it.

However, it was an inevitable that it would come to Michael's notice as he was a control freak who majored in covering all possibilities when planning a covert operation. He had put a minder on Allan Phair that included monitoring all his diary movements and the good doctor's decision to have a golfing weekend on the Isle of Man raised eyebrows. His suspicions were justified when he found that Allan had booked a double room at a 5-star B&B in Port Erin under a false name but hadn't followed it up by booking a starting time at any of the island's six golf courses.

All this created a dilemma for Michael as he feared 'pillow talk' could lead to his exposure destroying both his proposed attack on the Scotch whisky industry and more importantly his freedom. It was time to rendezvous with PK. Rather than meet at his house they arranged to get together in a quiet location in the countryside on the shores of Lough Neagh near Masserene where they would pose as ramblers out for a Sunday afternoon stroll rather than terrorists planning the assassination of an academic in Edinburgh.

Michael drove into the car park at Toombridge as the late morning sunshine glinted off the vast surface of Lough Neagh. There were a number of cars parked alongside with various parties going about their leisure pursuits, organizing everything from football matches to squeezing into wet suits before getting their boards ready for a bit of wind-surfing. He looked for PK's Volvo but there was no sign of it and he was glad to have time to reflect and plan his strategy for today's discussions.

Ten minutes passed before PK entered the car park at speed and brought his car to a halt, twenty-five yards away from Michael's Peugeot. He quickly disembarked and headed in t Michael's direction. "Sorry I'm late. The wife decided at the last minute to meet my eldest daughter in town for a coffee. "He explained, before shaking hands with his colleague.

Michael responded, "No problem I was enjoying seeing all these young people enjoying themselves and wishing I was still their age. Are you all set for a piece of rambling? I thought we could head in the direction of Ballyronan and take in the wildlife before stopping for a pub lunch at a hostelry I know in the Ballyronan Woods."

"Sounds good to me. I'll just get my anorak out the car and take it as a precaution although the weather does look settled." PK returned to his car and was back within the minute. "Lead on Michael."

The leader and his chief henchman set off in the direction of Ballyronan and mingled with other occupants of the car park, exchanging pleasantries about their home life until they found themselves on a wooded path with no one in earshot.

Michael opened the discussion, "PK, I have been able to examine all the evidence regarding what went on over in Birmingham both from the video you saw and the report that Mhairi issued to me. Her version of events as we know differs regarding Phair's conduct towards her, but as far as the information she extracted from him regarding the security procedures of the Scotch whisky it appears to be spot on. I have a copy of her report with me that I will let you read over lunch; better still let's sit down on that bench over there by the water and I'll let you read it now."

The two men planked themselves down on the green bench and Michael produced the five pages of type from his inside pocket and passed them to PK to scrutinize as he watched a couple of windsurfers demonstrate their skills on Lough Neagh. PK took a few minutes to absorb the report, grunting agreement and disapproval, as he did so before putting the pages back in order and returning them to Michael.

"But do you think you can still trust her Michael? If you want to continue with your plan to extort a ransom from Westminster she is a definite security risk."

"Come let's continue our walk." After a few strides Michael continued, "Well it's worse than that - I have had the both of them under close surveillance and my contact in Edinburgh tells me that Allan has planned a 'golfing weekend' on the Isle of Man staying at B&B in Port Erin. However, he has left himself open to suspicion by not booking any golf tee-time reservations at any of the island's six courses."

"He could have booked them under McClure." PK suggested.

Michael waved his arm in protest "No I thought of that and checked. Nobody had booked starting times under McClure. Golf is well down his planning agenda for the weekend - unless Mhairi proves too strong for him and he needs a rest. Based on the evidence to date they are well suited when it comes to carnal matters. As you can imagine this is very concerning and I am undecided as whether or not to proceed with my plans. Any thoughts PK?"

"Michael, this is very bad news. As I see it, it would appear we are threatened by the lovebirds. Mhairi is party to your intended assault on the Scotch whisky trade and if she becomes overly familiar with Allan Phair, she is liable to drop her guard and discuss confidences which could lead to our group being exposed and all of us facing the rest of our lives in jail."

"We have a decision to make. "Do we eliminate Allan Phair and if so how, where, and when? "

"My thoughts are that we have little choice for the reasons I have just mentioned," reflected PK, "I don't know Mhairi as well as you do. The very idea of a knock on the door from police or MI5 is the difference between her having a slip of the tongue whilst cavorting with the Scotsman, frightens me to death.

This elimination of Allan Phair would have to be carried out on the Mainland, Edinburgh most likely, as we do not want to attract attention to Northern Ireland. Michael do you have any timescale in mind? - when are the couple due to meet up on the Isle of Man?"

Getting out his diary Michael confirmed, 'Not until the autumn break, their accommodation is booked for two nights commencing Monday October 7th.'

"So that gives me seven weeks to get a plan of action in place. I will require all your data on Phair, where he lives and works, whom and where he socializes, what kind of car he drives and a copy of his diary. I will be using a team of my top professionals, some who may already be resident in the UK as this will make our exit strategy simpler."

"I'll leave the detail to you PK but obviously I will have to see a copy of the plan before you carry it out. I think we should keep this execution to ourselves otherwise there is more chance of a leak as some of our executive may have sympathy for Mhairi."

"How do you think she and the rest will react Michael?"

"Not sure, but she knows the score and the dangers of having an affair with the enemy. The others will recognize that there is always the risk of collateral damage when in an operation of this magnitude so I am not overly concerned."

"Changing the subject, we're nearly at the Neagh Inn, where I am suitably informed you get a great Sunday lunch and having sacrificed breakfast in anticipation I'm bloody starving."

Thirty seconds later PK placed his huge right hand on the brass handle of the restaurant door, stood aside and ushered Michael in. A waiter approached, but before he could open his mouth PK informed him, "Table for two please. Charge it under Caldwell as he", pointing to Michael, "is paying!"   Chapter 16

SEPTEMBER 1998

The traffic in Edinburgh's South Bridge was heavy as Allan Phair exited the quadrant of Edinburgh University before he turned left into Chamber Street. Shielding himself from the rain he crossed the road passing Blair Street before entering into the College of Arts car park where he had permission to keep his car. He was enjoying the sudden evening calm of being out of the traffic and paid little attention to the only other person around, the vagrant who had just limped past him. He had recognized the man as he had passed him a couple of nights earlier holding out a grimy hand and appealing, "Please give me something to help quench my thirst."

As he had done on the previous encounter Phair dismissed the beggar with a wave of his hand and was oblivious to the fact that the beggar had followed him into the yard. The beggar touched Professor Phair on the shoulder and when he turned round he was forcefully grabbed by the throat with one powerful gloved hand as the other clenched hand held a five-inch blade which he sunk into the professor's chest half a dozen times in quick succession. As the mortally wounded professor sunk to his feet the assailant removed his wallet and watch, closed his jacket and propped him up against a wall in a sitting position. He opened a nearby large waste refuse container, removed some sheets of cardboard from inside it before replacing them with Allan Phair's body. The corpse was quickly covered over by the excess garbage so as not to make it obvious at first sight to anyone tipping in new batches of litter.

The execution was over in seconds and taking the professor's attaché case, 'the beggar' moved off quickly, running down Blair Street, which had no CCTV coverage, into the Cowgate where a motorbike was waiting to remove him from the crime scene. The motorbike rider handed his passenger a helmet and took off in the direction of the Queen's Park. He stopped briefly just after the crossroads at Jeffrey Street, to allow the murderer to pass the murder weapon and the attaché case to an accomplice posing as a backpacker. He would later scrutinize its contents before disposing of it. The motorbike continued on down past Holyrood Palace into the Park in the direction of Meadowbank. Just past St. Margaret's Loch, the biker took a right turn up the hill, climbing up into the wastes of Arthur Seat the 900ft. extinct volcano that dominates the Edinburgh skyline.

The driver found a sheltered spot and switched off his lights. Quickly his passenger removed his false beard and make-up, changed out of his rags into a smart suit, collar and tie which had been in the pillion bag. Within minutes the professional assassin, whom the 1972 Club had hired from the London area, was ready to be dropped off at Duddingston Village where he picked up a car that had been planted earlier. He was soon driving down the A7 to join his 'wife' who had booked into a

hotel in the Borders. The motorcyclist headed for the Bypass on
route to the safety of Glasgow before heading to London the next day.

Chapter 17

Three days later Leith Police Station received a call from the Seafield Waste Depot reporting that a body had been found crushed in one of the refuse lorries. Detective Inspector Grant McKirdy was put in charge of the investigation assisted by Sergeant Neil Lamont who had been first to the murder scene. "Morning Neil, what have we got here then?"

"A body in the bin, Sir but in this case a refuse lorry has crushed the life out of it. We will not know the cause of death until 'Dr Death' (as police pathologist Willie Cowan was known), has done an autopsy."

Next day Willie Cowan had completed his examinations and phoned D.I. McKirdy, "Grant, Willie Cowan here, I've finished my autopsy on the body in the bin. I think you better come down and see me. This does not look like a case of accidental death, similar to what has happened in previous refuse lorry crushing incidents."

"Thanks Willie, we'll be right down."

After putting on surgical gowns the police officers entered one of the examination rooms and stood round the stainless-steel table beside the shrouded body of Allan Phair. Willie Cowan towered over the table. A tall man, he cut a portly frame with soft blue eyes topped with a thatch of silver curly locks.

"Morning gentlemen, this as you will see is not what we expected" he said pulling back the sheet to reveal the dead crushed corpse with punctured holes in the chest and abdomen.

"My God!" exclaimed the police officers who had been expecting to see a mashed body but not stab wounds.

Dr Death went immediately into reporting mode. "As I said, not what we expected. The torso has been flattened by the impact of the crusher but the victim was dead before he met that fate. Six punctures to the heart and intestines were administered which would have instantly rendered the victim dead. The weapon was a five-inch serrated knife but the metal pattern would indicate it was manufactured in Eastern Europe possibly Czechoslovakia. The killer was very professional, buttoning up the victim's jacket to keep the blood spillage to a minimum before he placed the body in the waste container."

"Motive" continued the Detective Inspector.

"On the surface, it would appear to be a mugging as the victim's watch and wallet are missing."

"Oh Christ," lamented D.I. McKirdy, "We'll have to trawl through missing persons before we can get started on our investigations."

"No that won't be necessary" interrupted Cowan, pointing at the corpse, "This is the remains of Professor Allan Phair of Edinburgh University with whom I have enjoyed many a convivial evening at the Staff Club in Chamber Street"

"A local man?" enquired Sergeant Lamont.

"Yes, he lives up in the Braid Hills with his wife Hilary, who is also an academic, and his two boys." answered the pathologist.

"Well we better arrange to meet Mrs Phair and see if she can shed any light on why anyone would want to kill her husband" Turning to his sergeant, McKirdy continued, "Get your constables to find out what they can about Allan Phair - his employment, hobbies, friends etc. so that we can build a picture of him and his whereabouts in the last forty-eight to seventy-two hours. Right I'm off to see Hilary Phair with PC Maggie Wright."

The Phairs lived in the wealthy suburb of the Braids in a very large stone built villa accessed by a loose stone driveway. McKirdy rang the bell at the side of an imposing large black gloss painted door with polished brass handles. Within a few seconds the door opened and an attractive brunette in her early to mid-forties, dressed in brown cords and a camel V-neck sweater looked apprehensively at her visitors.

"Can I help you?" she enquired.

"I'm D.I. Grant McKirdy of Lothian & Borders CID and this is my colleague PC Margaret Wright. Could we come in please?"

"Yes" stammered Hilary, "Let's go into the drawing room."

They were shown into a bright well-furnished room overlooking a lovely garden and invited to sit down on a blue Paisley pattered sofa opposite Mrs Phair, who curled up into an armchair.

Grant cleared his throat before commencing with a statement he had used many times before; - "Mrs Phair, I'm afraid we have some very bad news. Your husband Allan is dead. He has been mugged and his body dumped in a refuse vehicle."

A deathly scream emitted from Hilary Phair's lips followed by uncontrollable sobbing. D.I. McKirdy signalled to PC Wright to comfort the new widow. Several minutes passed before Mrs Phair regained her composure allowing Grant McKirdy to continue the interview.

"What happened to Allan?" the distraught Mrs Phair croaked.

"We don't know exactly. His body was found by workers at the Seafield Refuse Depot. It had been compacted in one of the refuse vehicles but on examination at the mortuary it appears that he had been the victim of a savage mugging and had been stabbed to death."

"Why the hell would anyone do that" asked Hilary in a loud sobbing voice.

"Well, we were hoping you might be able to help us, by giving us some information on your husband's lifestyle. Did Allan have any enemies or anyone that would bear a grudge against him?"

Hilary Phair hesitated before replying, "No!!"

Wiping away tears and taking a deep breath, Hilary began her revelations to the constabulary. "Inspector, Allan and I live, sorry lived, a very sexually liberal existence. Whilst we loved each other and looked after the family we both engaged in extra marital affairs and

116

attended swinger parties with some of our close academic friends. I am only telling you this because you will probably find out during your investigations but I cannot think of anyone who bore a grudge against Allan. He didn't come home the last two nights but that is not unusual as he often attends functions straight from work or gets delayed overnight with one of his lady friends."

McKirdy, taken aback by Mrs Phairs's honesty cleared his throat before asking "Are all your 'partners' local?"

"No", replied Hilary "they are contacts we have made over the years with whom we usually meet up several times a year at different large country mansions, throughout the UK which we hire for the weekend. We are careful who we admit into our circle but there have been no new admissions in the last two years. I don't think that any of our circle will be under suspicion. I have been honest with you and in return I would expect the police to respect my privacy and not ask for the identities of my group unless it is absolutely necessary."

McKirdy nodded. "I cannot give that guarantee but admire your frankness and will see where the investigation takes us, before answering to your request. Nevertheless, I shall require the names and contact details for all the members of your group so that we can eliminate them from our enquiries"

"Thank you, officer. I shall get my diary and give you our friends contact details," At that point Hilary left the room and returned shortly and handed over the slim red diary to PC Wright.

Grant McKirdy continued questioning Hilary Phair about her husband's character whilst his assistant wrote down the contents of the diary. When she stopped writing the D.I. signalled to PC Wright to close the notebook and brought the interview to an end finalizing the proceeding with, "We'll not take up any more of your time today and once more please accept our condolences."

Hilary Phair replied, "Please call on me at any time if I can be of further assistance. I want the swine who did this to be brought to justice."

At that point, the police officers headed for the door and drove back to police headquarters. On the drive back to headquarters, McKirdy turned to his assistant and asked, "What did you make of that, Margaret?"

"I was quite shocked by what Mrs Phair told us - she seemed so broad minded - I didn't think that sort of thing went on in the sleepy suburbs of Edinburgh."

"Not a lot, as a well-known magician would say, but can I ask you to be discrete and not discuss this with your fellow officers at this stage?" "Yes Sir" came her reply.

The D.I. entered his office at Leith Police Station and after looking briefly at his mail made his way to the suboffice to seek out his assistant DS Neil Lamont.

"Anything out of the ordinary jumped out of the page at you yet, Neil?"

"Yes sir," responded Lamont, "I have established that Allan Phair was based at the Old College building of Edinburgh University on the South Bridge but he parked his car over at the College of Art in Chamber Street. It has not moved from there in the last few days. Close to

118

the car there are a number of large refuse bins which were emptied earlier the same day on which Allan Phair's body was found at the Seafield dump. I have arranged for forensics to go over both the car and the refuse bins."

"Good work Neil" congratulated the D.I., "Anything else to report?"

"Yes, the doorman at the Art College spoke of a beggar with an Eastern European accent being seen in the area in the last few days. We are searching for him to eliminate him from our enquiries. Something I did notice was that the killer had buttoned up the victim's jacket after stabbing him which is something you expect from a contract killer rather than an amateur. I thought we should speak to the other police forces around the country to see if they have any tip-offs regarding contract killings."

"I'll speak to the boss and get something moving along these lines."

"Thanks sir. How did you get on breaking the news to Mrs Phair?"

"Let's get a cup of tea and I'll tell you all about it."

Once the tea and the obligatory digestive biscuits had arrived, McKirdy outlined his meeting with Hilary Phair and watched Neil Lamont's jaw drop when he reached the part concerning the academic swingers.

"We have a list of all participants whom I need you to contact. Due to the nature of their activities and the thought that the press would have a field day if they knew about this, I am limiting any knowledge of their

119

activities to you and PC Wright. I suggest that you carry out the interviews together as we do not want any backlash from these 'free spirits' which might damage any prosecution when we catch the culprit. Always remember Neil that the Edinburgh academic circles have contacts in high places. They can call upon favours from their friends in government to prevent the Establishment from washing their dirty linen in public. The chances are that someone on that list will be able to lead us to whoever was responsible for Allan Phair's premature and horrible end."

"I'll get on to it Sir, right away, but looking down the list this is going to take time as they are spread all over the country."

"I appreciate that" replied the D.I., "but I'm afraid it is necessary."

The next day the two detectives packed their bags and set out on a carefully planned strategic route to confront 'Hilary's List' as they had named the academics. Allan Phair's death was the top news item on all the media channels with a number of old sages paying compliments to the fine work the good Doctor had carried out through his contribution to both the food and drinks industry throughout the world.

It was several days before Neil and Margaret had completed their investigations. They arranged their appointments with 'the Swingers' and as part of their routine investigations into Allan Phair's murder, always made a point in having the both husband and wife present. During their conversations, they made it known to the interviewees that they were aware the extramarital activities as a means of loosening their tongues. This worked a treat and they were able to build up a picture of the victim's lifestyle and eliminate his friends from their enquiry.

One of the last meetings involved a visit to Inverness to meet Bob Ritchie a history lecturer at The Highland University, and his wife Angela. The meeting took place at the Ritchie's substantial stone villa that stood overlooking Inverness and the Dornoch Firth beyond. Bob Ritchie, a tall slightly overweight fifty-year-old with a head of spiky grey hair welcomed the officers into his home. After Sergeant Lamont and PC Wright had shown their warrant cards Bob opened the conversation.

"Glad you found us okay. You'll be wanting a cup of tea after the long drive up the A9. Let's go through to the kitchen where Angela will be putting on the kettle."

Angela Ritchie, a small brunette was a slim very fit looking lady who clearly paid a lot of attention to her appearance. "Pleased to meet you. Tea or coffee?" "Tea please" the officers answered simultaneously.

"Please, take a seat." Continued Bob.

The kitchen was a big bright room with a conservatory extension that looked out over a large beautifully laid out garden consisting of lawns, shrubs and flowers.

"Just talk amongst yourselves for a minute while I get the tea ready." said Angela.

The next few minutes were filled with talk of horticultural experiences or not as in bachelor Neil Lamont's case. Angela then placed the tea on the round oak kitchen table and Neil Lamont commenced his interview.

"Your friend Allan Phair met a horrible death as you know early last week and we are trying to piece together his last movements and what a possible motive there could be for his murder. Naturally we are leaving no stone unturned, so if there is any small thing you can think of that may be relevant, please tell us."

Hesitating, as he had done previously when addressing other members of the 'swingers club' Neil continued. "To cut to the chase I think it only fair to inform you that we know about the sexual habits of your group but are not treating their activities as part of our investigation at present."

Neil's statement brought an embarrassing smile to the faces of the Inverness couple and five seconds of silence prevailed before Angela spoke.

"D.S. Lamont thanks for being so frank with us. We had heard from our friends that you were aware of our meetings but it still makes one a little hot under the collar when the law exposes it to you in person. In our case we got involved with the others purely through socializing at academic events and the fact that we are unable to have children, made us decide to live life to the full.

I have always looked forward to the meetings and Allan was one of the main reasons for that, as he was an attractive man and all the ladies looked forward to spending time with him if you get my gist."

Bob piped up, "Mrs. Phair also played her part admirably."

Neil continued, "Was there ever any fallouts amongst the group which could lead to anyone holding grudges? Did Allan Phair curtail his straying from the marital bed to his friends or did he have any other dalliances that you know about?"

Angela Stewart replied first, "We have strict rules amongst ourselves that we are only interested in pleasure and anyone straying from that concept by way of being argumentative or confrontational in any way is asked to leave. Isn't that so Bob?"

Bob nodded, "Yes. As for how Allan conducted himself at other times, it is fair to say that he liked to chase the women. If I can give you an example we were at the University Staff Conference (USC) back in March in Birmingham. After the daily seminars are out the way, we party at night and Allan latched on to a very attractive lady from Antrim to whose room he ended up in. Next day however she was not seen until the evening and did not give Allan the time of day." "Do you think that she could hold a grudge?"

Bob shrugged his shoulders, "Who knows?"

"Do you know this lady's name?"

"Give me a minute and I'll look at the USC notes." Bob left the room but returned a minute later, "Here it is, - Mhairi McClure, Head of Computer Studies at Antrim University."

Sergeant Lamont's eyes lit up, "Thanks that could be very useful."

Several days later the ten-man murder squad sat round the large oak table in the conference room at Leith Police Station as D.I. Mckirdy opened the proceedings:

"Morning Gentlemen we are now nearly two weeks on from the killing of Allan Phair without any positive conclusion and as you can imagine I am getting it in the neck from Superintendent Anderson. So, what have we got to report? Albert, you start."

Albert Downing arranged his papers, clearing his throat.

"Well Sir, my team have been following up on the vagrant who was hanging around Chamber Street in the week before the murder but we have been unable to get a positive identification as to who he is. We spoke to our contacts in the homeless community and they have given us a description of the suspect which equates to that given by the university staff. Apart from this scant information we don't know much about him. None of the local hostels have any record of him seeking refuge for the night and nobody recalls sharing either a drink or any conversation with him. All this makes me think that our assassin is a contract killer. But why murder a university professor who specialist subject was grain development and protecting the good name of Scotch whisky?"

"Thanks Albert, I think you could be right about the contract killer. Neil, you were looking into Allan Phair's background. How did you and P.C. Wright get on?"

"We have had our eyes opened by certain aspects of the dead man's character.' Lamont smiled at his fellow team members before continuing, 'The Phairs are members of a swingers' club whose members are all academics dotted round the country. They meet several times a year at various country mansions which they hire for the weekend. Mrs Phair was open about their activities. I asked if there was anyone who would hold a grudge against Allan Phair but she didn't think so. She supplied us with the names of all the participants and having spoken to them all, our conclusion is she's right. Allan Phair was very popular with the ladies."

"So, no success there then Neil." sighed McKirdy.

"Not quite Sir" returned Neil, "Bob Ritchie up in Inverness told us about an incident at a University seminar down in Birmingham back in March where Allan Phair had a fling with an Irish lecturer from Antrim University which seemed to end with them falling out, so there is a chance that she may have held a grudge against him. With your permission, I would like to go over to Northern Ireland and interview Mhairi McClure."
"Okay, may be worth a call," approved D.I. McKirdy.

Chapter 18

EasyJet Flight EZYB6HY touched down at Belfast International Airport where the Royal Ulster Constabulary   had sent two plain clothes officers to meet Sergeant Lamont and PC Wright. After exchanging pleasantries, the investigation team made their way to Antrim University. Thirty minutes later they arrived at the security gate protecting the students from the outside world and told the guard they we here to see Mhairi McClure and were given directions to the

Computer Campus. In the meantime, the Northern Ireland acquaintances remained in their car.

A receptionist showed the Scottish detectives into a meeting room where coffee and biscuits had already been laid out. After a few minutes, a smartly dressed Mhairi McClure entered the room wearing a navy-blue business suit which was offset by a white silk blouse.

"Sergeant Lamont, I presume." smiled Mhairi.

"Yes, and this is my colleague DC Margaret Wright."

"Pleased to meet you both. Did you have a good flight this morning?"

"Actually no; it was a bit bumpy" contributed Margaret, "But the man next to me said this often happens due to the short journey and the plane flying at a lower altitude."

"Well let's hope the return journey is better."

The trio settled down at the table and Neil opened up his folder and began the meeting.

"Mhairi, we're here this morning as you know because we are investigating Allan Phair's tragic death. During our discussions with some academics your name came into the conversation and we have come across this morning to see if you can throw any light on why someone would kill Allan Phair."

Mhairi's facial expression grew as she exclaimed, "I hope that you are not suggesting that I had anything to do with Allan Phair's death. I only met the man once at a USC Conference!"

Neil held up his hand to calm the situation, "Miss McClure we are not saying that - but one of our interviewees told us that you and Dr. Phair had enjoyed an evening together. He detected that the next day you didn't seem to want to know him. What we are trying to do is piece together a picture of Phair's lifestyle and connect it to anything that might be a reason for revenge."

"Sergeant, you're digging a hole for yourself, but you are correct in that I did have a one-night stand with Allan Phair. We met in the disco at the Forest of Arden Hotel and danced the night away. Everything went well and we went back to my room where things got out of hand." "How?" PC Wright asked.

"Allan wanted to have sex but I said no as it was the wrong time off the month. He...he would not accept that", continued a now very embarrassed professor, "and forced himself on me. Allan Phair.... raped me!!" Mhairi blurted out before bursting into tears and sobbing into a handkerchief which she took from her handbag.

Silence engulfed the room before Lamont enquired "Did you not report this. Men like that should not get away with ravishing women."

"Next morning, I was so distraught that I stayed in my room all day, using room service for my meals. Late in the afternoon the Chancellor, Michael Caldwell, knocked on my door to enquire about my health as I had called off from the conference with an upset stomach. When Michael saw me, he knew something was wrong. I broke down and told him what had happened. Allan Phair had treated me roughly and left his teeth marks on my upper body and I revealed them to Michael."

"Oh my god, how awful," interjected PC Wright, "What a horrible character this Allan Phair must have been."

Neil Lamont continued "Our investigation has not as yet led us to any distinct reason for his death. One theory is a jealous husband. Did you know that he was a member of a swingers' club consisting wholly of academics?"

"Really!!" a shocked Mhairi replied, "I thought that was the sort of thing you read about in the tabloids. No, he never mentioned it."

"The rotten bastard." she thought.

"I'm very sorry to have put you through this again and we shall treat your evidence with the utmost confidence. To finalise my report would it be possible to have a word with Michael Caldwell."

Moving towards the telephone Mhairi replied, "Just a minute I'll see if he is available."

The officers heard the phone ring at the other end and a voice answering "Chancellor Caldwell."

"Chancellor, Mhairi McClure here. I have two officers from Lothian & Borders police who are making enquiries into Allan Phair's death and would like you to confirm aspects of my evidence. Are you available to talk to them?"

The voice replied, "Give me ten minutes and I will join you."

True to his word the Chancellor appeared wearing his black gown over a charcoal grey pinstripe suit offset with a white shirt and maroon tie.

Neil explained how the enquiry was going and why he had come over to Northern Ireland to see Mhairi. D.C. Wright read out her statement and when she finished D.S. Lamont turned to Michael Caldwell for confirmation.

"Is that an accurate description of events as you recall them Chancellor?"

"Regrettably yes" Michael replied softly, "a very sad encounter."

"Tell me sir, did you not think to press charges against Phair"' enquired the Edinburgh detective.

"Mhairi and I did discuss it but she had been traumatised so much that the thought of facing the world's media made her want to cover up the incident. In light of what you have told me about Allan Phair's private life it may be a blessing as the media would have raked Mhairi and my fellow academic colleagues through the gutter."

"Yes, I can understand that, but did you not have a word with Phair about his abuse of one of the members of your staff?" pressed D.S. Lamont.

"No, because Mhairi did not want me to and I respected her position." he lied.

"I don't think there is anything else to record," finalised D.S. Lamont, "So we shall head back to the airport."

"Before you go Sergeant, have you no thoughts on who would have carried out this dastardly deed?" asked The Chancellor.

"Between these four walls it is looking more and more like a contract killing. But so far there is no evidence to support this theory." Lamont concluded picking up his briefcase.

After seeing the officers off the premises Michael and Mhairi returned to the meeting room.

"Well Mhairi, I'm sorry you had to go through that ordeal once again and hopefully that is the last we shall hear about it."

Mhairi retorted "I don't like the thought that the police suspect a contract killing. Why would anyone want to kill Allan?" She then hesitated before confronting Michael Caldwell. "I take it this is nothing to do with our movement or your plan to attack the Scotch Whisky trade."

Michael was not ready for this quick analysis of Allan Phair's death and his body language gave him away.

"How could you, you bastard!" she screamed, "Allan was not a threat to you. He was a decent guy whose company I enjoyed and whom I might have liked to meet up with again."

"In Port Erin in the Isle of Man no doubt." scoffed Michael with a defiant look in his eye.

"How do you know about our planned rendezvous in Port Erin?"

"I make it my business to know everything about my team Mhairi. There's no way I was allowing my plans to be revealed in a moment of high passion. I've worked too hard for the last thirty years for it all to end by pillow talk."

Mhairi looked Michael Caldwell in the eye before threatening "Michael, I'll not forget this and remember I can use this conversation to go to the police and turn you in at any time."

Michael delayed his response before replying in a cold steely voice; "I think you would be very unwise to contemplate any such action as you would be the one who would come off worse. I had your room at Forest of Arden bugged with a CCTV camera as I had originally planned to blackmail Allan Phair. I have in my possession a CCTV video of the nocturnal proceedings that occurred in Room 216 at the Forest of Arden hotel. Actions that you lied to me about and almost made me arrange for the elimination of the Scotsman then. I did give him a verbal warning but obviously that did not deter you going behind my back and further deceiving me by arranging a weekend in Port Erin. So Mhairi you have, by your actions, brought Allan's death upon yourself!"

Mhairi's face went white with rage and her knees buckled under her when Michael added by a means of confirming his revelations, "I liked your Irish wolfhound position. Any further insinuations or thoughts of talking to the police regarding the Allan Phair murder and I will release the video to a larger audience which would finish your career and standing in Irish society."

The Chancellor then left the room and his sobbing and distraught colleague.

Chapter 19

Seamus Carr's mobile phone vibrated to reveal that 'X' was calling him. 'X' was Michael Caldwell's code name and he only used that phone line for important business.

"Hello. Yes, I know the promenade at Port Stewart, I'll meet you at the Ice Cream van. Two o'clock on Friday afternoon."

Seamus arrived early in Port Stewart and had a walk before he spied Michael approaching the ice cream van and getting himself a 'Mr. Whippy 99 cone' with a Cadbury's chocolate flake in it. Ten seconds later Seamus made a similar purchase before the two of them strolled off along the promenade. Seamus opened the conversation.

'It's a lovely afternoon so it is, a lovely sunny Autumnal afternoon with people all relaxed and preparing for the weekend. So, what is it that brings you here Michael?'

After taking a lick of his ice cream Michael responded, 'Seamus, I mentioned some time ago that I wanted to reap revenge on the British by targeting their economic infrastructure and that I have been working on a plan to put the first of these attacks into place. The chosen target is the Scotch whisky industry as it's a significant revenue provider for the British government. This strategy may make them think of abandoning their policy of not paying monetary ransoms to terrorists as they like to brand us. My plan is long-term and may not come to fruition for some time yet but I have to put the structure in place now to achieve my objective.

My research to date has demonstrated that there are security systems in place that would make it difficult for us to attack our target through the front door. So, what we need is someone working for us on the inside. You have lists of all our 'sympathisers' so what I want you to look for is one who can implement our plan.' Seamus interrupted, 'And what is our plan Michael?'

'At this stage, Seamus it is MY plan but should you find me the man I want I will quickly divulge to you and the rest of the team how it will operate.'

Finishing off his ice cream and wiping his mouth with a pale blue handkerchief Seamus summarised, 'All right, I'll see what I can do. I'll get the girls to go through the membership and report back to you. We'll meet here again but next time the ice creams are on you.' Michael shook hands with Seamus, 'It's a deal.'

During the next few days Seamus' team searched their records with a remit to look for a sympathiser who lived in Scotland and was employed in the whisky trade. They were not hopeful of completing their task successfully and could not believe it when only a few hours into their research they found someone who ticked all the boxes. John Gourley, a fifty-two-year-old originally from Strathane.

John Gourley had been attracted to Edinburgh after he had met his wife at a dance in Glasgow when he had gone to watch his beloved Celtic play in the semi-final of the European Cup at Hampden Park. The 'Bhoys' won 2-1 and John and his mates made their way to the

Barrowland Dance Hall where he met Pauline Dolan from Edinburgh, the love of his life. After a year of going back and forward between Strathane and Edinburgh the couple married at St. Pauls The Evangelist Roman Church in Portobello and set up home in Bingham, a council estate on the east side of the city.

John had worked as an agricultural labourer in Northern Ireland and found it difficult to pursue similar work in Edinburgh. After a few unsuccessful interviews, he landed a job at Scotia Distillery which was one of the few remaining grain distilleries in the centre of a city. He soon learned all the menial tasks in the distillery, which included detailed knowledge of the spirit store where they filled the casks with one hundred and twenty per cent proof white spirit. The casks were then despatched to a bond to lie for a minimum three years before maturing into Scotch whisky. John became knowledgeable of the workings of his department and was respected by both his colleagues and the management but not being Scottish or Protestant he was never given the promotion he deserved. This annoyed him and led him to dipping into the warehouse casks, opening the bungholes and extracting samples which at first, he consumed in moderation but which later escalated into a serious drink problem.

In the early years of their marriage the Gourleys regularly returned to Strathane every summer for their holidays as, with three young children to feed, money was tight. However, the children had now flown the nest, but between low wages and John's drinking problem, they had never been abroad. Having ageing parents John still managed to return to Strathane to visit them on his own. When he was there he would have a

134

night out with his pals at Strathane Republican Club where they served up cheap drink.

Seamus Carr made enquiries about John Gourley's allegiances to the republican cause and whether after living for so long out of Northern Ireland he had mellowed. Feedback was that he was disenchanted with his work and if his wife agreed he would return to Strathane when he retired but that was still more than a decade away. He and Pauline, who were both staunch practising Catholics, had one ambition however, to visit the Vatican and be present at the Pontiff's Sunday address to his followers. Seamus slowly built up a picture of John Gourley which he presented to Michael Caldwell for discussion.

Michael bought the ice cream as expected and the two gentlemen walked a short distance along the promenade before sitting down on at an empty bench. Seamus put his hand into his inside pocket and produced an A4 envelope that he passed to his leader. Michael rapidly read the document and then addressed Seamus.

"So, Seamus what makes you think that John Gourley is the right man for us after taking into account his present employment position?"

Seamus moved uncomfortably in his seat before replying, "Apart from the facts that you have before you Michael, I have mingled with some of his relatives at the Republican Club and they told me that prior to meeting his wife in Scotland he was involved in IRA activities to help our movement. His contribution was not of a violent nature so he never came to the attention of the British. He was regarded as one for the future and many thinks had he remained over here would have developed into a first-class soldier."

"But true love intervened", commented Michael, "does he still have leanings towards us?"

"'Yes, some of his friends are in senior positions within the movement and they assure me he would have continued to assist us. Obviously, I don't know what you have in mind Michael, unless you are prepared to divulge your plans to me. We can't be seen to pay him large sums of money but I have thought of a way we can use him for your plans."

Michael cast a quizzical look at his colleague, 'Continue.'

"The Gourleys are desperate to visit His Holiness at the Vatican and although there is no chance of getting him close to the Holy Father. I could speak to my local diocese and get them some private blessing as well as prime seats for Papa's address to the masses at St.

Peters. Getting them over to Rome is not a problem. Down at the club we periodically run a big raffle with a first prize being an all-expenses trip to the Vatican and I'll fix it that he wins."

"How will you do that?" the academic asked.

"Chairman of the Republican Club is a very lucrative position. If he was holding a draw, the second prize would be a Rolls Royce - the first being a place on the committee!"

Michael laughed before answering "Point taken Seamus, arrange a meeting with John Gourley next time he's over. I'd like to meet him and satisfy myself he's the man for the job. I can't release any further information to you at present and when we do meet up with Mr Gourley we will speak to him covertly as I do not want him knowing our identities. Is that understood?"

"Of course, Michael, good point. I will follow the same procedure when I am making the arrangements for the raffle draw."

"Okay Seamus. Time to go, these clouds look as though they are carrying a good soaking which I don't need falling on me."

The men made their way to their respective cars and never met again in Port Stewart for ice cream.

Chapter 20

NOVEMBER 1998

John Gourley arrived in Strathane to visit his parents and was met as usual at the airport in Belfast by his boyhood friend Tom Comerford. After pleasantries, the pair set off for Strathane and Tom started up a conversation;

"How are things in the Capital of Scotland John? Still making good money to look after the family?"

John grunted back, "You'll never make money in the distillery although they are fair employers but its dead man's shoes - unless I decide to join the Freemasons." He joked.

"Fat chance of that with your previous, helping the Cause like you did. Have you ever wondered how things would have turned out had you stayed in Strathane? I mean you were one of the brighter recruits when we were youths. I've continued on from those days and now make a good living from paramilitary activities compared with being a plumber, but I still do a few 'homers' when asked."

"Aye Tom, it would be great to have a bit more cash but Pauline would never agree to come back here. We've been away too long."

"The reason I mention it was your name came up in conversation with one of the local commanders Seamus Carr and he said he would like to meet you next time you're over. I don't know what he has in mind but it is well known that the local commanders like to have a network of spies on the mainland feeding them back information and supplying safe houses when required."

John reacted, 'Well, I suppose it wouldn't do any harm to talk. With Pauline having stayed at home I'll have time on my hands during the day.'

Tom smiled and replied, 'I'll phone Seamus after I've dropped you off and see if I can set up a meeting.'

Ten minutes later the car pulled up outside the Gourley's council house on the McFee estate, one of the less salubrious areas of Strathane. Tom retrieved John's luggage from the back seat of his car and followed John into the house. The door opened and the diminutive white-haired figure of Mrs Gourley, wearing a brown woollen jumper and black trousers was standing there stunned. She let out a shriek of delight which awoke her husband who had been sleeping on his chair. 'Tim! Tim! Johnny's here! You're looking weel son' she continued as she embraced John and kissed him as only a mother can.

The Gourleys were a close family and Tom Comerford stood admiring them and wished that his own parents had not passed away a few years ago. He laid down John's bag and then excused himself telling John that he would phone to arrange a time to meet him in the Republican Club. Once clear of the McFee Estate Tom pulled into a side street and phoned his commander, "Seamus good day, how's it going? I've just picked up John Gourley from the airport and delivered him to his mum's house. I spoke to him about meeting up with you and he's all for it. It would be better to have it during the day as he'll be out on the piss with me every night!"

"You said he's only here over the weekend until Monday so I'll try and set it up for lunchtime tomorrow. Thanks Tom, well done and I'll be in touch later today." Seamus concluded.

Michael Caldwell received the phone call he had been anticipating from Seamus and arranged a rendezvous at 20 miles from Strathane in case any of the locals recognised him or John Gourley being seen together in the same neighbourhood. The farm was owned by Anthony McCloskie, who had diversified his premises by offering training facilities for agricultural students. They only attended five days a week, so this suited perfectly as no one would be around to witness the 1972 Club leader's visit. Tom and Seamus Carr plus 'escorts' picked up John Gourley in a Ford Galaxy with smoked glass windows. They had no sooner left the town when Seamus produced a black hood.

"Here John put this on. The hierarchy do not want you to know where the meeting is being held."

John looked at the hood in disbelief, "Tom, are these guys getting carried away. You've known me all your life and this seems a bit over the top." "Sorry John, we're just obeying orders."

When their vehicle arrived at the farm it was driven straight into the barn. John was led into a room and had the hood removed. He found himself in a room with a wooden table and four matching padded chairs to match. On the table was a bottle of water and plastic cups. Tom left the room and John sat facing the CCTV camera in the corner.

Next door Michael Caldwell had been joined by Seamus, PK and David Cossar who were all going to be involved in the next phase of the operation. Mhairi McClure and Colm Murphy would play their parts later in the planning process. The four discussed their line of questioning before switching on the CCTV and the intercom connected up to the room next door.

Michael opened the discussion, "Afternoon John, pleased to see you and thanks very much for attending this meeting. What we are about to discuss is highly confidential and should not be related to anyone, including your wife, as you will be aware having served with us before. The reason we have asked you here today is because the politicians have signed up to the Good Friday Agreement which will affect how we conduct ourselves in future."

"Yes, it's a real bastard, so it is, for we who seek to run our own destiny and want to break away from the British" interjected Gourley.

"Quite so, John" continued Michael, "This has made us look to ways of hurting the British economically and that is where you can help." All four committee members noted the quizzical look on Gourley's face before Michael resumed, "We have chosen to attack the treasury by wreaking havoc on the Scotch Whisky stocks and thus denting the revenues of the Chancellor of the Exchequer. We have done some research into the security systems currently in place within the whisky industry. It would appear that it is almost impossible to smuggle anything out, but the same is not true for taking anything in."

"How do you propose I do that?" asked Gourley.

"I'll come to that, but first I need you to confirm your allegiance to our cause because once you have accepted to assist there will be no retreat and failure to carry out your duty will be seen as an act of treason punishable by death."

Michael purposely paused there and let silence fill the two meeting rooms and waited for John Gourley's response: "I've always regretted in some ways leaving Ireland and living in Scotland where I am unable to serve my country. As the years passed, I have found myself under the same oppression that you have here in Northern Ireland which can be very frustrating. Job promotion opportunities do not come my way and so economically I feel I'm in limbo, not being able to give my family a better standard of living. So, it would give me a sense of pride and purpose to help the republican cause."

"Thanks for that confirmation John - now here's what I would like you to do for us and what we will do for you and Pauline in return. We would like to upset the British by threatening to destroy a major whisky installation in Scotland and the one I have chosen to implement my plan is in the Scotia Distillery where you work. I can see a look of panic come over you. No, I'm not planning on blowing up the distillery, it's too near the centre of Edinburgh and heavily populated areas which would result in hundreds if not thousands of deaths. What you can do for us however is, over several weeks, deposit small explosive charges into whisky casks that will be transported to various bonds around Scotland ready to be exploded if our ransom demands are not met. Am I right in saying that the employees are not searched when they arrive at your distillery for their daily shifts?"

A still shocked John Gourley slowly replied, "Yes, we clock in and then make our way down to the cooperage to see that all the whisky barrels are ready for the day. The spirit store operation has to be on schedule as any delays there will cause a backlog in the distillation process and bring the whole distillery to a halt. The same applies to the transportation, as no full barrels are allowed to stand out with the parameter of the spirit store to comply with Customs & Excise regulations. Once the teams are in place which is usually by 8.00a.m. the filling programme can begin. Customs & Excise place a 'watcher' in the store who puts a seal on the Crown Locked Vehicles (CLVs) prior to them leaving for their resting place at a bond. There is also a team of four Customs & Excise officers who roam around the distillery

142

checking the specification of the raw spirit or the strength of mature whisky which is leaving the distillery, destined for a blending house, and to make sure none of us have been sampling it early. As if we would do such a thing! So, what I'm saying is I could do what you want."

"Excellent John, we shall make plans to despatch six Semtex charges to you in the near future. We want you to place them in appropriate casks that are all bound for different whisky bonds so that we have a good geographical coverage, which will bring fear to the British government. How far in advance do you know where the casks for filling are being bonded John?"

John rocked back in his chair and took a swig of water before answering, "The Filling Programme is worked out every Monday morning for the white spirit being produced for use the following Monday. It is put together by the Office Manager and the cooperage foreman who has to know how many casks he has to produce. The office manager will inform his spirit clerk on the agreed programme for the week and he will then arrange for the bonding plus the transportation of the barrels. We usually get to know five days in advance when and where the casks are going."

"Not a big lead time but sufficient enough for us to pass the explosives to you. Tell me John, are the barrels completely empty prior to filling?"

"No, a small amount, usually 500 ml. in every fifty-sixgallon hogshead, of a sherry substance called Paxarette is added to each barrel before they are filled, to give the white spirit some colouring when it is lying in bond.", Gourley informed them.

"Good, that will help camouflage the small packages you put down the bunghole. See how I'm picking up the whisky jargon from you."

"On another matter, I understand you and your good wife Pauline would like to visit the Vatican. As a reward for assisting us we will inform you at a later date as to how we will make the trip possible. Do not however mention this to Pauline. We will inform you how we will make the trip possible. I think that is about all we need to discuss today but remember what I have said about confidentiality.' warned Michael Caldwell before eerily adding "I would not like to see Pauline becoming a widow."

"U... understood" stammered Gourley.

As he stood up a new voice that of David Cossar came into the room, "John, before you go tell me, do you like sausage rolls?"

"Yes, I do, - why?" replied John.

The question was answered by the sound system closing down.

Immediately the meeting finished Tom Comerford entered the room, placed the hood back on John's head and returned him to his car for the journey back to Strathane. After they had been driving twenty minutes Tom removed the hood.

"How did you get on John? I'm asking because I am not party to meetings at that level."

"I'm beginning to wish that I wasn't either, Tommy lad. So, we'll leave it at that if you don't mind", concluded a glum John Gourley.

Back at McCloskie's farm there was a short debrief of what had been discussed with John Gourley. It was agreed that the full committee would meet the following Saturday morning at the Chancellor's quarters in Antrim University where Michael would discuss the attack on the Scotch whisky industry in full. During the week Michael informed the group that he would be in touch so that they would come to the meeting fully prepared as to how they could fulfil their part of the assignment.

Chapter 21

The sun was setting on what had been a lovely Winter's day as Michael drove his BMW into Connaught Place, where the affluent residents of Belfast lived and parked it about a hundred yards from the entrance to the driveway of David Cossar's mansion. Michael pressed the doorbell that set off the barking of vicious sounding dogs, followed by the unlocking of the stained glass reenforced door. A very smart casually dressed David Cossar in navy blue chinos, yellow Boss sports shirt covered by a cashmere powder blue V-neck sweater ushered Michael into the sumptuous hallway. Cossar was in his early fifties, slim built with lank silvery hair which was slightly tinged by the number of cigarettes he smoked.

"Michael, let me have your coat and we'll go through to my study where we will not be disturbed." Looking about, Michael asked, "Where are the dogs?"

David smiled back, "There aren't any. It's a record to frighten off anyone who approaches the house when we're not in."

The pair entered the study and David took his seat on a leather swivel chair behind a large oak desk, while Michael settled into the leather seat in front of the desk.

"Before we start, Michael can I get you a drink or a coffee?"

'Normally I would say a Scotch but I'm driving, so a cup of tea would be fine David."

Picking up the phone on his desk David pressed a button and spoke to someone on the other end, "Can you bring us a pot of tea for two and some biscuits, please?"

"Lovely place you have here David, have you been here long?" Michael enquired anxious to make small talk until the tea had been delivered.

"We moved in about five years ago, we like it - there are seven bedrooms, four public, a swimming pool and an indoor tennis court. I have five kids so it keeps them all occupied. A bit different from the two bedroom flat I shared with six siblings when I was growing up. I've worked hard to get to where I am and will always be grateful for the part the republican movement has played in my success."

More small talk followed before a knock on the door preceded a young blond-haired girl entering the room carrying a tray with tea and biscuits.

"This is my daughter Alison who hopes to enrol with yourself in a couple of years' time. Alison, Mr Caldwell works at Antrim University." David explained.

Michael stood up and shook the girl's hand, "Hello pleased to meet you, what are you thinking of studying Alison?"

"Law and French Mr Caldwell" replied the shy teenager.

"Well, nearer the time get your Dad to phone me and I'll give you some advice about entrance procedures." Alison thanked Michael for his offer and left the room.

"Thanks Michael, now let's see how I can help you."

Michael opened his briefcase and took out some papers. "As I indicated I have a plan to extract money from the British by threatening to blow up a significant part of one of their cash cows, the Scotch Whisky industry. Research has revealed to us that it is possible, with the help of an insider, John Gourley, to plant explosives into casks of whisky which are due to be distributed to bonds around Scotland. Your expertise is in the weapons theatre an area of which I have little knowledge and I would like to hear your suggestions how we could achieve our target."

David took time to reply before commenting, "This is the first time I have heard of your plan and I think it is an ingenious one. There are some questions to be answered before I can proceed to ordering up the weapons.

1. Who will have control of the firing pins or have the final decision regarding the implementation of the explosives?

2. Are they going to be on a timer or will they be activated remotely?

3. What warning period is to be issued bearing in mind an explosion of this nature will cause devastation over a very large area that, if not cleared, could result in a large loss of life?" Michael took a deep breath before replying, "Regarding your initial question the final decision will rest with myself and two members of our committee who will be named later. Moving on, I would not utilise a timer as there could be mechanism problems resulting in them exploding early or not at all. So, they should be

fired securely from a remote distance. My plan is only to activate the explosives as a last resort if the British turn down our request for ransom money. However, after they have seen an example of our devices exploding they will be forced into red alert and all their civil defence facilities will be called into operation. So how would you suggest we go about planting the bombs David?"

"I listened to John Gourley very carefully and he appears to be able to move freely around the area where we would want to deposit our bombs. For this kind of operation, we would use Semtex as it is light and waterproof. I am not sure how white spirit coming off a still at one hundred and twenty proofs will affect it, but I would take the precaution of placing them in sealed plastic containers. I'll get our suppliers to check out the technicalities. We would only require a small device big enough to blow a hole through the cask as thereafter the surrounding casks stored in the bond will ignite and do our job for us. John mention that they put a brown syrupy substance, Paxerette, into the casks prior to filling. I would weigh our device so that it mixes in with the seasoning and remains static at the foot of the barrel, not floating about. All this planning is dependent upon John getting our explosives into the distillery and I've thought of a way of disguising them. You may recall that I asked John if he liked sausage rolls. The reason I asked is that we could camouflage the Semtex to look like sausage rolls so that if he was subject to a routine search he would be less likely to be exposed."

"Very clever David, I like the sound of that." said Michael pausing to scratch his chin, "The plan is to have all the explosives in place over a three-months period starting in a fortnight if you can meet that supply date, although we will not be issuing our demands until months later so as to surprise the British."

David responded, "Regarding supply, my contacts south of the border in Galway can have it here ready in seventy-two hours."

"Good let's leave it there for now and if you come up with any problems let me know. Can you prepare a short verbal presentation for the meeting on Saturday? I don't want anything in writing to hand out to others in case it falls into the wrong hands. I will however need a copy for my records."

Seamus Carr flashed his head lights in the direction of Bobby Cargill's car when it entered section D of the car park at Asda's in Lisburn. Bobby got out his car and made his way to the red Mazda 626.

"Evening Bobby, I thought you were never coming but I should have known. You'd be late for your own funeral. I wanted to touch base with you to make sure everything was in hand for the big raffle."

"Yes, I'll get Tom Comerford to buy some tickets for John Gourley and put the stubs for that book in a safe place after marking his numbers. I will be doing the raffle personally. When it comes to the big moment I will pick out a ticket and announce John Gourley the winner, before substituting the ticket I have picked out with Gourley's ticket, which will be in my pocket. That ticket will then be passed to a committee member for ratification."

"That sounds too simple. Are you sure it will work?" responded Seamus.

"Absolutely Seamus, we do it all the time" smirked Bobby.

Chapter 22

PK was in a brooding mood when he met Michael. The plan for the assault on the Scotia Distillery appeared a little flimsy to him as he did not have a 'hands on' part to play in the procedure. The pair met in a café where they purchased two carry-out cappuccinos for their stroll through Malone's Sir Thomas and Lady Dickson Park.

"A bit of a wind blowing today, Pat, but least it's dry for now' said Michael adjusting the zip on his jacket, 'I wanted to have a word with you before the meeting on Saturday to get your point of view on the plan we spoke about."

"I listened to all you had to say the other day but I must say I'm concerned that our plan revolves around outside agencies in the shape of John Gourley, who could shop us at any time, and we all spend the rest of our lives in prison so we will. Even after the bombs are planted successfully he could take fright and how are we going to stop his conscience from informing the authorities?"

Michael took a sip of his drink before responding, "That's where you come in Pat, I have arranged through Seamus for Gourley to win the raffle at the Republican Club which will take him and his dear wife off to the Vatican for a once in a lifetime holiday break. It will be your job to make sure he does not return."

That last remark stopped PK in his tracks. "Michael! I will not arrange to carry out any terminations in the confines of the Holy See, that's just too close for comfort. If anything goes wrong I would be excommunicated from the Catholic Church. I just won't be a party to that one. So, you can forget it."

"Calm down Patrick, I don't want to upset anyone in the Vatican either. Any 'accidents' we plan will be well away from the St. Peters area. I was thinking that that you would be using the same agency which carried out the Edinburgh killing although I would not want a copycat assassination which could be traced back to Allan Phair's removal. The Gourleys will be in Rome from the Saturday until the Tuesday, the highlight for them will be mass at St. Peters on the Sunday, which I think they should experience. So that leaves your team Sunday evening, all day Monday and part of Tuesday to plan their attack. It is unfortunate we have to resort to removing John Gourley but I, like you, want to sleep at night, knowing there will not be a loud knock on the door while I am doing so."

PK relaxed a little before summing up the situation "Okay Michael you're right. This is a specialised job which I would rather pay to have carried out correctly. If I send any of my own team to Rome they will be flagged up at the airport but the London based hit men have the choice of transport and can go by air, Euro Tunnel or ferry if they want to make it a driving holiday. I'll talk to them and report back to you."

Michael replied, "That will be good Pat. There's no great hurry as Mr Gourley will not be winning the raffle for a few weeks. Come on, that's enough planning for now Pat, let's take a walk up to see Wilmont House, the big house on the hill over there. It was used to house Yanks during the Second World War, and they tell me there's also beautiful rose gardens nearby."

"Lead the way Michael."

Chapter 23

It was a dry windy Saturday morning on the Antrim Uni campus when the 1972 committee assembled at the Chancellor's office. Michael Caldwell produced a couple of thermos flasks, paper cups and a packet of digestive biscuits. Mhairi McClure played 'Mother' pouring out and distributing the coffee while engaging in a bit of banter at the same time. Everyone settled down and Michael called the meeting to order.

"Morning everyone and thanks for your attendance. During the week, I have had meetings with members of the committee but it is important that we co-ordinate our plans, so no one is in any doubt at what stage we are at and the contribution for which individual members are responsible in the context of the master plan. USQUABAE DE AUG, which is Gaelic for water of death, is the name I have chosen for the plan to topple the Scotch Whisky industry. Whisky is described in Robert Burns's excellent poem Tam O'Shanter as USQUABAE (Water of Life) with which Tam would face the Devil!' But enough of the literary lesson. In no particular order David, would you like to start us off."

"Michael and I met at my house during the week. He explained his plan and the need to place explosives into whisky casks using John Gourley who works at Scotia Distillery. I have suggested we use Semtex which will be camouflaged to look like sausage rolls", stated David to a chuckle form his colleagues. "I have been in contact with my explosives supplier in Cork and they are preparing the consignment for delivery. They will arrange to have it

154

delivered into Scotland and then arrange to pass it to Gourley, who will let us know when it is required."

Michael continued, "I want John Gourley to spread the explosives throughout the country to small and large bonds. If the British wants to call our bluff I will give them the cask number of the cask which is placed at the smallest bond so that they can call out the bomb squad and verify our threat."

"Good thinking Michael, let the bastards sweat, this could make the Birmingham Bull Ring bomb look like a picnic without the loss of life and condemnation which it produced." said Colm Murphy.

"I'm very aware that we all want to ensure there is no mass murder Colm. Now Seamus, bring the others up to date regarding John Gourley and how and when we can make use of him?"

"John was over here recently as you know. Michael, David and PK conducted an interrogation without showing their faces and using sound equipment to disguise their voices. I wasn't in the room but I got the impression he is going to co-operate. John has a desire to go to Rome and as a way of rewarding him I have arranged for him to win a special raffle being held at the Strathane Republican Club with a first prize of a weekend in Rome" The faces of the others in the room transformed into a relaxed smile before Seamus went on "All I need from you Michael is when the plan is to come into operation."

Michael was quick to re-act "I cannot confirm timings at present. This plan will take months of preparation and you will all be taking on different aspects of the implementation process. So, don't be surprised or feel left out if I come and say to some of you that we're in place to start negotiations with the British. Obviously my two fellow dons, Mhairi and Colm, will be particularly involved in the final stages especially finding a home for the ransom money."

After his recent confrontation with Mhairi, Michael was very reluctant to feed her too much information in case she was still determined to reveal to the authorities her information regarding the death of Allan Phair.

David Carr raised a finger to interrupt, "How does that work Colm? "

Glancing at Michael, Colm replied, "There are a number of trails used by the drug cartels and money-launderers with which I am familiar with but you will appreciate I can't go into any detail about these. When I was working in the Golden Mile I ran across a few unscrupulous contacts who were involved in moving Arab and Russian fortunes around the world so I don't foresee any great difficulties. As long as the world's governments conduct a futile policy of allowing all the little principalities like Luxembourg and Monaco, not to mention Switzerland, deal in financial clandestine transactions, we'll be able store our booty with little difficult."

Michael was looking at his watch as Colm finished his contribution "Well I am conscious that I have brought you all out on a Saturday morning and that we all would like to take advantage of the lovely sunny weather outside, free from the rain that's dogged us for the last few weeks. So, has anybody got any questions?"

Everyone looked round the room at each other before PK, who along with Mhairi had not spoken at all, raised his hand.

Michael acknowledged him, "Yes PK."

"Nobody has mentioned security. Am I right in saying that I will be responsible for all aspects of security and I will have direct control over all logistical elements of the plan? Naturally I will be working closely with you all and will be reporting directly to Michael. An assault of this nature requires highest priority code 'Green' meaning, as you know, any security leaks are punishable by death." PK coldly stared around the table and the others in the room nodded their agreement without making eye contact with the IRA hit-man.

Chapter 24

DECEMBER 1998

"Hail! Hail! The Hibs are here!" chanted the fans in Middlemas Bar, a busy Easter Road hostelry prior to their game against Celtic. John Gourley positioned himself in a corner so that he could watch out for 'Kevin the Delivery Man'. He had been told Kevin would be wearing a green and gold badge on his Hibs woollen beanie hat. The door opened and a small slight figure in the apparel described to John entered and made his way to the bar scouring the patrons as he did so for John Gourley. After waiting five minutes for his pint of

Belhaven Best he made his way over and stood next to his fellow countryman.

"This could be a tough one for us," said Kevin, "I've travelled from Northern Ireland today to see the match."

John Gourley's eyes lit up, "Where are you from in the Provence?"

"A small village you might not have heard of Strathane?"

That was the password John had been given so he wasted no time in introducing himself, "John Gourley" extending an outstretched hand.

"Pleased to meet you." Replied Kevin without revealing his identity. "Let's take a seat over there. I'm starving, fancy a sausage roll?"

John felt himself get hot under the collar at the thought of taking possession of the disguised sticks of Semtex, "We'll have to go to the baker's up the road for that."

"Okay, drink up and you can take me to where they sell the best carry-out food." Leaving the pub, the pair made their way down Easter Road mixing with the football fans before taking a left into Iona Street in the direction of Leith Walk where Kevin had parked his white van. He unlocked the sliding side door and invited John to join him. Inside the interior was laid out like a small workshop with a work-bench, seating and tools fitted neatly in ranks on the walls.

Kevin sat down and carefully opened a package that revealed six sausage rolls neatly individually wrapped. John stared at them mesmerised by the detail of the disguise and simultaneously, felt concerned as to how he was going to handle them. His hands started to sweat at the very thought of the damage these deadly small packages could inflict upon the community.

Picking one up Kevin said "Don't be afraid of Semtex. It's a very flexible explosive we have acquired from the Libyans as it is waterproof. I recommend you drop the whole package in the cellophane cover down the bunghole as it is weighted and will float down to the bottom of the cask. There is a detonator placed in the Semtex but it will only be activated by remote control on the orders of the High Command. When do you expect to commence your part of the operation John? "

No reply. Kevin raised his voice into a low shout "John, when do you expect to get started?"

Waking out of trance Gourley mumbled, "Soon after the New Year, I'll place the first one then wait for instructions as to when they want me do the rest. I'm passing over information on all the filling programmes of where the casks are going for bonding and the idea is to spread them over as large an area as possible."

Kevin reached under the bench and brought out what appeared to be a metal biscuit tin, removed the lid to show that it had a special reinforced lining in the shape of the six pastries. He carefully lifted the contents off the table and placed them into the tin. "John, Semtex is quite flexible so don't be worried, it only goes off in extreme temperatures and I don't think you'll get much of that in Edinburgh."

"No, it is drier than Strathane but that bloody East wind is so cold it cuts through you."

Kevin continued "It goes without saying you have to keep it in a safe place. Where do you plan to store it?"

"Well away from my house. I've got a locker at the Niddrie Bowling Club that I have had for years, but hardly ever use but at least the explosives will be under lock and key."

"Does the club get many burglaries?"

"Occasionally but they're not usually looking for sausage rolls!" laughed John.

Chapter 25

JANUARY 1999

The festive period had passed and all the maintenance at Scotia Distillery had been carried out in time for the workforce returning to start the distillation process for producing raw alcohol. The labourers were not needed in the spirit store for a few days so John found himself working in the bonds despatching barrels out of the warehouse on their journey to the blending houses. There, their contents would be bottled for either export or the home market. The side benefit of the warehouse environment was the number of 'Samples' that were made available illegally for consumption by the workers. John resisted the temptation of a free nip as his mind was on more serious matters.

The Scotia Distillery had been turning out spirit since it started in 1850 and the three-hundred-foot chimney, now oil-fired, filling the skyline at the west end of the city had become an Edinburgh icon. Scotia concentrated on producing a Lowland grain whisky using the Irish Coffey Still method. The distillery employed over two hundred workers, almost half of whom were in the cooperage. Distilleries were money making machines for although there was a three-year maturing period before the spirit qualified as Scotch whisky the distillation process fed off plenty of bi-products. CO_2 gas, wet draft that was sold for cattle feed, dried grains bagged for chicken feed and exported overseas, fusil oil used in the production of cosmetics and even the damaged barrels were sold to garden centres for tubs. The distillers also had a fall-back position, in that they could convert the white spirit coming off the Still into gin which they could bottle instantly.

Every Monday evening Gourley sent a coded message through to Glasgow with details of the Scotia Distillery filling programme. Nothing happened for the first two weeks of the New Year then on a Wednesday night the phone rang and a voice said 'Put our first bet on the 200 hogsheads going to Hillfoots Bond No.2 on Friday morning for Aberfeldy Distillers.'

Friday January 21 1999 was a bitterly cold frosty morning with a moderate East wind to add to the discomfort. John Gourley's heartbeat raced as he stepped off the No. 4 bus and made his way down the Distillery Lane to the Scotia Distillery. John clocked in as usual at the gatehouse which was directly opposite a building housing the office staff and the Customs & Excise. He then proceeded on to the bothy provided for the spirit store workers next to the grain silos and changed into his uniform. Going into his satchel he brought out his Tupperware lunch box and opened it to reveal his usual sandwiches plus the 'sausage roll'. He was so nervous that he didn't notice Tom Downie his workmate entering the room. Looking over his shoulder, Tom declared "Well Johnnie boy Pauline is looking after you today, that's a nice-looking treat you've got today - I'll maybe get a bite of that sausage roll at lunchtime."

John managed to recover from his initial fright to mumble "Maybe, but I've not had my breakfast so I don't think it will last that long" He picked up the sausage roll and put it gingerly in his jacket pocket. He had worked out the best place to slip the Semtex into a cask was when they were all stacked up horizontally waiting to be brought into the Spirit Store for filling. Conscious of the CCTV he turned barrel No. 5378 on its side and, positioning it where the bunghole was not visible to the cameras, he inserted the deadly explosive before rolling the barrel into Spirit Store for filling.

The Spirit Store itself was a large shed that could host several hundred whisky casks. A large glass box housed two clerks who recorded and calculated the spirit content of the casks. They did this by deducting the 'Tare' -the weight of the cask when empty - from the full weight when it was rolled on to the weighbridge in front of them. Using tables in front of them they converted the net weight into volume gallons. At the far end of the spirit store there were two massive vats that each held ten thousand gallons. On the top of one vat sat Andrew Buist, the spirit store manager, at a high desk looking down on his department like the ship's captain.

Gourley watched nervously as the stainless-steel filling pump was inserted into the bunghole of cask 5378 and within seconds the white spirit filled its vacuum before a worker hammered a temporary bung into the bunghole.

The cask then joined the rest of the consignment bound for Hillfoots Bond No.2. Before this happened, a cooper replaced the temporary cork bung with a solid oak one that would remain there for the distillation period of at least three years. Over the next three months John Gourley repeated this routine sending a further five casks to bonds of varying sizes around Scotland as follows:

FEBRUARY 6 No. 7367 to ALVA BOND 8, CLACKMANNANSHIRE

FEBRUARY 21 No. 9612 to KINNOULL STREET, PERTH

MARCH 3 No. 11085 to BOND 9, SHETTLESTON, GLASGOW

MARCH 16 No. 13212 to LUNDIN BOND, LEVEN

MARCH 24 No. 15527 to BALLANTRAE BOND, GIRVAN AYRSHIRE

Thus completing the first part of Michael Caldwell's Master Plan.

Chapter 26

MARCH 16th 1999

"Jack, we've got a problem there's a leaking cask - No. 13212." Willie Duffy informed his fellow spirit clerk Jackie Cockburn.

"Okay put it to one side. Get the lads to use one of the casks from the next batch as both consignments are for James Stalker Distilleries. The Customs watcher is anxious to get the Crown Locked Vehicle outside secured and not have any transportation backlogs. I'll go and see Jake the cooper and get him to attend to the racker." concluded the slim Cockburn.

Jack got a hold of the Spirit Store cooper Jake McGowan, who had one of the labourers move the leaking cask to one side of the spirit store while he rolled across a stainless-steel vessel with a suction tube. Taking a piece of white chalk out of his pocket he put an 'X' on the leaking stave. Removing the bung, he placed the tube into the cask and drained the contents into the vessel. Turning the cask on its end Jake slackened off the steel hoops then removed the end before replacing the cracked stave that was causing the leak and inserting a new one. Looking into the barrel McGowan spotted the wrapped Semtex parcel lying amongst the brown paxerette slurry and being curious he scooped it up. 'How did a sausage roll get in there?' he mused to himself before dropping it back in rather than walk thirty yards to the closest rubbish bin. The cask was then renumbered as No. R13336, refilled and weighed before joining the new consignment bound for Lundin Bond near Leven to be bottled sometime in the future under the James Stalker Distilleries label.

Jake McGowan was no stranger to putting objects down the bunghole, having once cornered a wayward rat that strayed into the filling area. Using a sack that he threw over the unfortunate beast, he then grabbed it and forced the rodent down the bunghole - before drowning it in fifty -four gallons of one hundred and twenty proof

164

white spirit that in future would be sold as pure Scotch Whisky!

While the racking repair was taking place John Gourley was enjoying his break over in the canteen chatting to his workmate Stan McGill and was totally oblivious as to the current whereabouts of the bomb he had recently planted in what he thought was in cask No. 13212 which had now been re-numbered R13336.

Chapter 27

APRIL 10th 1999

Addressing the 1972 Committee Michael Caldwell began:

"I am pleased to inform you all that on March 24 John Gourley completed the task of planting explosives in six whisky casks that have been despatched to bonds throughout Scotland. These bombs will lie there for some time as I think we should be in no hurry to discharge them. We are just eight months away from the Millennium celebrations and I would use this as a countdown to make the British Government sweat by making our demands known nearer the end of the year."

"Hopefully January 1 2000 will have a very lucrative outcome for all of us. I would like to thank David Cossar and his team for getting the first phase of our operation into place. Before we proceed, Colm and Mhairi will assume that our plans will come to fruition and organise safe havens for our spoils which can't be traced by the British. How long will that take you Colm?"

Colm adjusted his seating before answering, "Michael this will entail a very large number of financial transaction. So, I will need to utilise several routes to process it effectively. I would recommend we use a number of tax havens all over the world from Bermuda and the Cayman Islands to the ones nearer at home such as Luxembourg, Lichtenstein and Monaco. The funds will only be in the banks for as long as it takes for them to be cleared and then we shall request they be exchanged for U.S. dollar notes in high denominations. Local security companies will collect the funds on our behalf and take them to a safe haven ready to be transferred and 'cleaned' by a third party." Colm indicated stretching his arms in the air and bending his forefingers as he made this statement.

Seamus Carr was so mystified by Colm's confidence of pulling together a global coup that it led him to ask, "Colm, are you sure this will work? Won't the British be able to shadow the money?"

"Oh, they'll try" Colm responded and brought an embarrassed smile to Miss McClure's face by continuing "but Mhairi, our computer genius and I have been very successful to date in shaking them off our trail by using fictitious companies. We have been transacting our illgotten gains this way for several years. Are you okay with that Seamus?"

Seamus laughed "Yes, it's all a bit above me so I'll stick to working out my Travellers Cheques for our fortnight in Majorca."

The meeting continued dealing with local issues for another hour before Michael Caldwell brought it to a halt and wished everyone a pleasant afternoon.

As the group was leaving the office Michael singled out PK and asked him to stay behind. Closing the door, he leaned back on a chair before addressing his hit man. "PK, you'll see I have left quite a time lapse between the explosives being planted and negotiations commencing with the Blair government. The others are not to know this but this is to give us time to implement a plan to eliminate The Gourleys."

"Michael you'll have to watch out that Seamus Carr keeps his mouth shut after he arranges the date for the Grand Raffle at the Republican Club. We don't want him ruining our plans."

"Well PK, I rather thought that was more in your territory as a word in his ear from you will put the fear of God into him."

"All right Good Cop', smiled PK, 'I'll play bad cop."
Chapter 28

NOVEMBER 20th 1998

John Johnston spoke in a soft Northern Ireland accent, "Hello, can I speak to Mr Hugh McFaul please? Tell him it's George Best on the phone."

"I beg your pardon Sir, did you say George Best, THE George Best" the lady telephonist enquired.

"Only joking. My name is John Johnston, I'm a friend of Mr McFaul and I am calling from Johannesburg South Africa."

"Really Sir, this call must be costing you a fortune. I'll put you straight through to Mr McFaul right now."

Seconds later John heard the receiver being lifted and to his surprise a voice with an upper-class English accent answering, "McFaul, how can I help you?"

"Christ Hughie, what's with the upper crust accent? It's me that's been out the country for years and I still retain my Irish tongue when I'm talking to family or close friends."

"John! Great to hear from you. Sorry about that, but Irish accents are not welcome here in the Ministry of Defence. Are you in London now that you've recently qualified as a doctor? Are you phoning me to see if there are any vacancies in Harley Street?" Hughie jested.

"No, I'm phoning from the house to tell you that I am coming over shortly with the Old Jeds Rugby team to play a couple of games and see the Boks thrash England at Twickenham. Only problem is I haven't been able to get a ticket yet. Any chance of getting one through the British military?" John enquired.

"My boss is a keen rugby fan. He's Scottish, so he might not be too fussed about watching an England v. South Africa match, but he is Chairman of the Army Rugby Association and has access to tickets. Leave it with me and I'll see what I can do. I take it you still have the same mobile number."

"Yes, Hughie" John replied.

"When do you arrive in the U.K.? We must have a night out, I haven't seen you since I visited you in Jo'burg in 1995 for the Rugby World Cup."

"Oh, the one we won, smirked John before continuing, 'I arrive on the 28th November and leave December 8Th. We have games on November 30th and then the 1st and 4th December."

"Tough Schedule John, hope you are ok to see the Twickenham match." Laughed Hughie.

Three days later John received a call on his mobile as he was unpacking a bag in his room at The Holiday Inn near London Bridge.

"John, Hughie here", no upper class accent this time, "Well as they say in South Africa 'Your bum's in the butter.' My boss was in a good mood when I spoke to him about having a Springbok as a guest on Saturday. In fact, he went even further and has invited you and me to a pre-match reception under the stand."

"Fantastic McFaul does it again! I don't suppose you've fixed us up with a couple of your best Mata Haris' for the evening. What time do I have to arrive at Twickenham and what is the dress code?"

"12.30. Come to the Main Stand entrance, the game kicks off at 3 O'clock and you will require a jacket and tie."

"Pity! I was all set to turn up in my Safari Suit", joked John, "look forward to Saturday, bye for now Hughie."

John Johnston strode confidently through the doors of the main entrance at Twickenham Rugby Stadium to be met by a commissionaire, "Afternoon Sir how can I be of assistance?"

"I'm here as a guest of the MOD for pre-match lunch, Sergeant McFaul should be waiting for me."

"Well Sir, if you would like to register with that young lady over there" replied the officer, pointing to a smartly dressed redhead overseeing a table of name cards in front of her.

John approached and announced "John Johnston, I'm a guest at the MOD table."

The receptionist scanned her table before picking up a label and handing it to John, "You're on Table 12. Some of the other guests are here already enjoying drinks in the bar including Sergeant McFaul. If you go up the stairs to the first landing and turn right that will take you into the bar area."

John entered the bar and was taken aback by the throng of people and the vocal racket they were creating. After jostling through the crowd for twenty seconds he spotted Hughie, approaching him from behind he tapped his shoulder, which caused Hughie to spin round.

"John, you've made it with your face still in one piece - the body swerve must have improved! Let me introduce you to our fellow table guests. I'll not mention ranks unless I have to." Turning to the immediate company Hughie announced to all "this is John Johnston, my oldest friend, who has travelled all the way from Johannesburg to see the Boks get their just deserts this afternoon!"

John smiled and retorted, "No way, No way! We are the Champions of the World!"

Hughie was about to continue with the frivolity but glancing over John' shoulder he replied "Ah, here's the boss."

John turned and met the blue eyes of a plump man in his late forties with thinning fair hair, who for some reasons seemed familiar.

Hughie made the official introductions, "John this is my commander, Colonel Colin Inglis."

John held out his hand, "John Johnston, pleased to meet you Sir"' he replied in his best clipped South African accent.

"The pleasures mine. Good to have you with us, as long as your team doesn't win." he replied bringing his right hand out of his trouser pocket, which with two fingers missing, made it awkward to shake hands. The Colonel sensed John's surprise but continued holding up his hand, "War wound, I was shot in action during a tour of duty in Northern Ireland in 1982."

"Sorry to hear that Colonel." John managed to reply hiding the sick feeling in his stomach as his mind recalled the crime he had witnessed, carried out by his host for the afternoon - Colonel Bloody Colin Inglis!

During lunch John was very quiet, his mind churning over the events of the past. The massacre of the soldiers, his banishment from Northern Ireland to South Africa and the assassination of his father- all caused by the man laughing and joking across the table. The Colonel had led an entirely different existence - fast tracked through MI5 as a result being excused front line duties due to his 'bravery in action'.

John could not wait to get home to see his mother and reveal to Claude Van Rensburg his real reason for coming to South Africa. Claude could then set up a meeting with Stanley Laab of Mossad, the only difference this time would be that he would also attend, to give an eyewitness report of what had occurred so many years ago.

Hughie had noticed the change in John's demeanour and was so concerned that he followed John to the toilet, "Are you okay John, not like you to be so quiet when there's free drink about."

John looked at himself in a mirror and saw that he was a bit pale, "Sorry Hughie, I was just thinking of how our lives had turned out and how my Dad would have loved to have seen us still friends after all these years." he lied before adding with a smile, "I will stop being melancholy now as it's time for the Boks to take England apart." England won 13 – 9.

Following on from the rugby John and Hughie went on to a fashionable bar in Clerkenwell where Hughie had a number of friends waiting. John was still simmering from his meeting with Colonel Inglis and wanted to question Hughie about his boss. When they were half-way through their third drink John began his crossexamination: "Your commanding officer seems a nice guy. What's he like to work for? "

Hughie took a swig of his beer before replying "A bit different from how he appeared today. He's a stickler for discipline and a bit of an ogre in the office?"

"Do you think that stems from the fact he lost two fingers in action? Where in Northern Ireland did it happen?" pressed John.

"Maybe, but he never talks about. There is a veil of secrecy as to where he lost his fingers - no mention of it on his CV- but one of his contemporaries told me under the influence of drink that it happened in 1982, very close to our village. Imagine that, who would have thought there were ops being carried out near us"' Hughie ended.

"Does he live in London Hughie?"

"Colonel Ingles has a lovely pad in Primrose Hill where he lives with his girlfriend who comes from a really moneyed family. So, he lives the high life and is a member of several of the Establishment's best clubs in London."

"Returning to your earlier comment about Special Operations being carried out near our houses, it's a small world Hughie" John said sarcastically. Raising his glass, he asked his friend, "Time for another pint?"

"Sure thing John, and this time get me a packet of crisps as well."

Chapter 29

At 7.30p.m. South African Airways flight SA2334 landed at the re-named Johannesburg International Airport and ten minutes later John Johnston descended into the warm evening air - a far cry from the shivers of London. After clearing customs, he was greeted by his mother and Claude, then forty-five minutes later he was back at Rivonia in the family home. During the journey, he gave a resume of the rugby tour and no mention of Colonel Inglis.

As the housemaid Jane made them coffee Claude excused himself and headed for his study. This gave John the chance to speak to his mother about his Twickenham experience. "Mum, you know I went to Twickenham with Hughie as a guest of the MOD. I got a real fright when I met Hughie's boss Colonel Colin Inglis - he is the same officer who shot dead three of his own soldiers and was responsible for the death of the American Matt O'Reilly and three IRA members."

"What!! Are you sure?" shrieked Joan so loud that Claude came charging into the room.

"What's going on? I thought we had a burglar."

Linda looked sheepishly at John before she answered, "Claude, John has made a devastating discovery in London and it's quite unbelievable. Take a seat, you'll need it when we tell you what really happened all those years ago, hence the hurried arrangements for John coming to live with us in South Africa."

Claude listened to John, as he emotionally translated the events he witnessed as a twelve-year-old and then described his meeting with Colin Inglis in London and how he shaken hands with the three fingered Colonel. When he finished Claude asked, "What do you want to do now?"

Tears welled in John's eyes, "That man was responsible not only for me coming to South Africa but also for the assassination of my Dad. Dad had seen something he shouldn't have on that disc which contained references to Matt O'Reilly, linking him to IRA activities and died because of it. I would like revenge on Colonel Inglis but have no idea how I could achieve it."

Claude responded, "I think I do. I will set up a meeting with Stan Laab and get his advice, but this time I will get him to come here so we can discuss it in complete privacy. We can give Jane and Tom the day off when he visits."

John thought, "Just the response I had hoped for."

On a beautiful sunny Highveld morning Stan Laab, wearing a cream safari suit, arrived at the Van Rensburg residence in Rivonia and pressed the security bell. The big electric gates opened slowly allowing him to drive up to the large white thatch -roofed house where Claude was waiting for him.

"Beautiful Morning Claude. Lovely place you have here." began Stan as he got out of his Mazda SUV.

"Yes, we're very lucky. Been here ten years now and I wouldn't change it for anything. Being such a nice day I thought we should sit out on the patio. I've given my staff the day off so our meeting will be private. Follow me Stan."

Stan obeyed Claude and walked through the impressive centre of the house out on to a large patio with space for a big table surrounded by eight bucket-shaped basket chairs. The end of the patio had an open staircase that led down to a beautifully manicured garden with a twenty-five-metre swimming pool constructed in the middle of it.

John and Linda were already sitting at the table and rose to be introduced to Stan. After handshakes Linda offered everyone a choice of coffee or ice-cold fruit juice. Claude opened up the dialogue "Stan, the reason for asking you over this morning is that there has been a further development regarding the information I gave you several years ago - unbeknown to me I might add.", stated Claude. In a serious tone eyeing the other members of his family, "Its best if John explains." The young man hesitated before beginning:

"Mr Laab, in 1982 prior to coming to live with my mother in South Africa, I witnessed the shooting of seven men. I had been playing football with my friend Hughie and was returning to the house through a path in the woods

when I saw four armed British soldiers hiding. My Dad had always told me to hide when armed soldiers were about and not make a sound, so I did just that.

A Land Rover appeared and one of the soldiers fired a shot into one of the vehicle's tyres causing it to come to an abrupt halt. Three armed men got out of the vehicle along with a younger man in a blue jacket. I couldn't believe what happened next, the three armed occupants of the Land Rover were gunned down but I never heard a shot being fired."

"They'd be using silencers." contributed the Mossad man, "carry on."

"The young man, the sole survivor of the massacre at this stage was in a state of shock when a soldier who appeared to be in charge approached him. He started screaming at the soldier in an American accent how the British should get out of Northern Ireland. The officer responded in a sarcastic tone and the young man made a dive for a gun nearby but he too was assassinated. The officer was fuming because the young man was not to be harmed. After issuing instructions the soldiers fired off a few rounds using their enemies' guns, after which they laid down the weapons and relaxed. It was at this point the officer picked up an automatic pistol and ended the lives of his own men."

Stan Laab couldn't contain himself, "Are you sure about this John? Why would he do such a thing? I find this quite incredible and frankly hard to believe."

John's face went red with embarrassment and His mother intervened to protect her son, "Mr Laab this is not the end of the story and I can assure you John is not one for fabricating things."

"There's more Sir. Afterwards the officer who was wearing gloves, re-arranged the weapons and made a call to his command centre telling them how everything gone wrong, he needed assistance because he had been shot. He ended the call, picked up a pistol in his left hand, aimed it at his right arm and fired. The bullets hit his right hand removing his forefinger and middle finger before he passed out. This gave me time to make my escape back to the house. I explained everything to my Dad who was worried that everyone, the British Forces, the IRA and the family of the American Matt O'Reilly, who had connections to the Boston underworld, would be searching for information and I could be in danger from them."

"Now, fast forward to my recent trip to London where I attended The England V Springboks rugby match at Twickenham as a guest of the Ministry of Defence courtesy of my friend Hughie McFaul. Hughie introduced me to his commanding officer who I thought I recognised from my past. It was confirmed when he shook hands with a right hand that only has three fingers. I knew immediately that he was the butcher of my youth. His name is Colonel Colin Inglis and he now works for MI5!
And that's it really."

A flabbergasted Stan Laab leaned back in his seat pondering what he had just heard, "So what do you want to do about all this?"

Claude replied for John, "Having discussed this as a family we would like to bring Colonel Inglis to justice but don't know how to go about it and thought you could advise us through your connections."

Stan replied "This is a very complex situation which you have witnessed, if you exposed it through the media it could lead to an international incident as an American citizen was involved. Then of course the Irish will be up in arms, the UK government will deny everything unless the media provide their information source which of course then exposes you and puts your life in danger. These are only my immediate thoughts, but leave this with me and I will liaise with Tel Aviv, get their advice and come back to you. I will however need what you have told me in writing. Do I have your permission to send over my assistant to take a statement from you John?"

"Certainly, whenever you want, I'm on holiday for another week so anytime would suit." John replied.

"Thanks Stan, for giving your time this morning it's very kind of you." said Claude on behalf of his family.

"No bother Claude" replied Laab before turning to John, "You, have been very unfortunate young man, having your youth destroyed by the dark forces of war and I will see what I can do to rectify the situation."

Driving back to his office on the East Rand, Stan Laab began to analyse the revelations he had been privy to and how that information could be used by his movement. Mossad could decide when the time was right to reveal the secret file on The 1972 Club to MI5 in exchange for 'favours' in the Middle East. Alternatively, they could threaten to expose Colonel Inglis through the media sparking off a crisis in international relations and protests from the families of the British soldiers he had killed in cold blood. Then of course there was the O'Reilly family in Boston who would also be interested in hearing about Colonel Colin Inglis. "Yes," finalised Laab, "It's been quite a day, a good intelligence gathering day, for the Israeli Secret Service."

Chapter 30

FEBRUARY 1999

On Saturday February 13th 1999, the Republican Club in Strathane was packed full for the Valentine Dance everyone wanting to win the chance to visit Rome and the Vatican City. At 9.30 precisely the drummer in the band smashed his cymbal to bring the crowd to order. Bobby Cargill, complete in his dinner suit, appeared on the stage with a microphone in his hand and began to address the crowd.

"Good evening all you lucky people, and who is going to get a romantic break in Rome complete with a visit to the Vatican itself to see the Papa? Without any further delay, I will make the draw." Approaching the raffle drum, giving it a roll before thrusting his hand into the transparent inners of the drum. Pulling out a ticket he held it aloft and announced to the assembled crowd; 'The winner of the trip to Rome where they will be put up for five nights in a three-star hotel and have £500 spending money is... John Gourley, 14 Bingham Broadway, Edinburgh EH15, Scotland!!"

The Chairman's announcement was met with complete silence followed by mutterings of "How did a bloody Scotsman get into the draw" and "he'll never know, draw it again!" until Tom Comerford reacted screaming "Jesus, I bought that ticket for John, the lucky bastard! I must go and get him on the phone to tell him the good news"' Comerford's outburst deflected attention from Bobby Cargill allowing him to complete his deception by substituting John Gourley's ticket and placing the one he had taken out the drum into his jacket pocket. After passing the substituted ticket to a committee member for ratification he left the stage and headed for the Gents where he entered a cubicle ripped the ticket into small pieces and then flushed it down the toilet. Mission completed.

John Gourley was sitting in the Niddrie Miner's Club when Bob the barman approached him to say his wife was on the phone. "Oh Christ, what's she wanting, can a man not have a drink in peace" he complained to his three boozing buddies as he headed to the bar to answer the call.

"Aye Pauline, what's wrong?" he barked into the headset.

"John, you'll never guess, your mate Tommy Comerford has been on the phone from Strathane. Remember he got you to buy some tickets for the Grand Draw? Well you've won first prize and we're going to Rome for a five-night stay that includes a visit to the Vatican for Sunday Mass at St. Peter's. Isn't that fantastic John?"

No reply was forthcoming as John was speechless and then gathering his composure managed to croak out through tears in his eyes, "Pauline that is unbelievable, I'll be right home to celebrate. Get your see-through nightie on," He laughed before replacing the receiver, saying goodnight to his fellow drinkers and making his way home with a skip in his step.

Next day The Gourleys received a call from Bobby Cargill confirming their good fortune. "When will the holiday take place, how do we get there and where will we be staying in Rome." asked an anxious John Gourley who held out the phone from his ear so that Pauline could share in the reply.

"The trip has been booked for Easter and you will be in St. Peter's on Easter Sunday. You're booked on a Ryanair flight that leaves Edinburgh at 11.45a.m. on Thursday morning and returns 2.00p.m. the following Tuesday. During your time in Rome you will be guests at Hotel Ontario, a three-star hotel ten minutes from Termini Station and close to Castri Pretorio Metro. God, I sound like a bloomin' travel agent. I'll send over the tickets to you in plenty of time and hope you enjoy Rome. If you have any questions just phone me on Strathane 1977. Bye for now, have fun." concluded Cargill.

EASTER WEEKEND

"Pauline, its April Fool's Day but the joke's not on us as we're on our way to Rome!" exclaimed John Gourley as he escorted his wife on to the Ryanair flight. After settling into the flight, the Gourleys had a couple of celebratory drinks to calm their nerves as neither of them were relaxed fliers. After landing at Rome's Ciampino Airport they took a train to Termini Station then walked from there to Hotel Ontario. The couple were shown to a large tastefully decorated bedroom complete with a beautiful marble en suite bathroom.

"Oh John,' said Pauline, "We are so lucky, I just can't believe it."

Across town two motorcyclists had just arrived at a local back-packers hostel. They had driven in from Ciampino Airport having been there to make sure their 'Targets' - John & Pauline Gourley - had arrived safely in the celestial city.

182

The next two days the Gourleys took in all the Roman tourist sights - St. Peter's Square, the Spanish Steps and the Trevi Fountain where Pauline made a wish that her family had lots of happiness. On Easter Sunday morning, they made their way to St. Peter's square in plenty time to see the Pontiff's address to the gathering masses. A pre-arranged rendezvous with a young Irish priest, Father Frank Rafferty had been set up and he had secured a special viewing position for them. Father Rafferty, had been sent to Rome to study and be ordained before deciding whether his future was in missionary work or returning to a parish in Ireland.

The Gourleys entered the Vatican by a side door shown into a large high-ceiling room where there were many fellow pilgrims enjoying coffee and sandwiches. Father Rafferty introduced them to other attendees, who not only spoke English, but were also working-class people who would have something in common with John and Pauline.

"Hi I'm Bert Cagney and this is my wife Joan, we're from Montreal Canada "said an elderly thick set bald gentleman in a light fawn suit edging his wife nearer the Gourleys. Joan was smartly dressed in a green floral dress that covered her rather overweight body. On her head, she wore a yellow wide brimmed sun hat.

John responded nervously shaking Bert's hand, "John and Pauline Gourley from Edinburgh Scotland, although I'm originally from Northern Ireland. We're here because I won the first prize in a raffle in my home town of Strathane and a local priest arranged for us to attend today's sermon."

"Is that right" exclaimed Joan, "Well I'll be damned! We've never been that lucky. You two must be on cloud nine."

Joan's friendly approach loosened Pauline's tongue and she immediately started telling the Cagneys all about their trip to date and they reacted with tales of their own Roman adventure. Ten minutes later a senior priest called the assembled company to order and directed them out into the Italian sunlight where they took their seats with an excellent view of the Papal balcony on which a few minutes later the Papa appeared to instant jubilation from the thousands of followers in St. Peter's Square. He spoke for about 20 minutes and his message for the day was a very poignant one, as it involved the Peace Process in Ireland and how church welcomed the coming together of the two communities in Ireland. John Gourley did not altogether agree with his leader's sentiments. After the Pontiff left the balcony the service continued for about another hour.

Everyone was overcome at seeing the Pope, no one more so than Bert Cagney, who suggested that the four visitors should celebrate with a drink then consider going for lunch. The Gourleys were up for this and it was not long before they were sitting comfortably in the Centurion Bar where Bert ordered a bottle of Prosecco. Pauline Gourley was not familiar with downing fizzy wine so by the time they had finished the second bottle she was quite giggly and loose tongued telling the Cagneys all the family secrets. Although they were very amusing, John was glad he had not devolved any information to Pauline about the forthcoming events planned for the Scotch Whisky industry. After a three-course lunch with more wine Pauline suddenly suffered the effects of the alcohol making her rush to the nearest toilet, quickly followed by Joan Cagney who tried to help her in her hour of need. John and Bert continued drinking until about half an hour later Pauline appeared ashen white prompting a 'Taxi for Gourley to Hotel Ontario'. As she got into the taxi John looked over his shoulder and whispered to Bert, "I'll get her settled in then I'll come out for a few more drinks so stay put so I can find you." 'Will do, fella', smiled Bert Cagney.

When the taxi arrived at the Hotel Ontario John was embarrassed to be helping his drunk wife out of a taxi at what was mid-afternoon on a Sunday when the streets and the hotel reception were busy with pilgrims. Not wanting to have a scene in the hotel reception area the hotel staff came to his rescue and quickly had Pauline in her room lying flat out on her bed. She was full of apologies, "John, I've ruined yer day by having too much drink and making a fool of myself in front of Joan and Bert who are such a lovely couple."

"Dinny worry, Pauline you're jist no used to sitting in the sun drinking that cheap fizzy wine" said John trying to console his wife.

"Your day's ruined John. Now I just want to sleep this off, why don't you go back and link up with the Cagneys, that's okay with me."

"Seriously Pauline, I must admit I was enjoying myself when we had to leave in a hurry."

Pauline Looked kindly at her husband, 'you're one of the best John Gourley, and deserve to enjoy this weekend to the full. So be off with you!'

Half an hour later John entered The Centurion Bar and was immediately shouted to by the Cagneys who were continuing their binge drinking session. "Is Pauline okay John? ", Joan enquired.

"Yes Joan, she's tucked up in bed but will probably have a sore head in the morning. She's not used to drinking sparkling wine, but the good news is she's given me a late pass so let's have some fun"'

The trio remained in the pleasant ambiance of the Centurion for another couple of hours by which time all three had a bit of sway on. This had not gone unnoticed by the two gentlemen who were sitting across the road awaiting their opportunity to dispose of the drunk Scotsman.

The weather had deteriorated considerably outside and the drunks were met by a violent thunderstorm and a very heavy downpour when they finally went outside.

"Quick," Bert Cagney shouted, "Find a taxi or we are going to get soaked through. I know a shortcut down through the Spanish Steps two blocks away."

The streets were still busy despite the bad weather as many tourists had been caught out by the sudden change in the weather. John led the way with Bert supporting Joan as she tried to avoid falling down. When he reached the top of the Spanish Steps at the Trienti Dei Mai John turned to see if the Cagneys were behind him but lost his balance on the slippery surface - his feet going up in the air away from his body. He came crashing down, smacked the back of his head on the marble steps, instantly breaking his neck, before his limp body continued to bounce like a rag doll down the surface until finally coming to rest.

Bert rushed to help his new friend but failed to get any response when he checked his pulse. A crowd had gathered which included a para-medic who put all her training to use but had to admit defeat to the forces of nature.

An English voice, belonging to one of the two assassins in the crowd asked "Is he okay?"

"I'm afraid not Sir," replied Bert.

"Damn it," thought the assassin, "We will only get half our fee for a job not completed." Then he and his colleague disappeared from the scene before the police arrived.

Chapter 31

Captain Luigi Arcari of the Rome Police responded to the 999 call and was quickly on the scene with two of his junior officers. The witness reports confirmed that the death was completely accidental and the Captain sanctioned the removal of the dead Irishman to the morgue. He was able to ascertain from the Cagneys the whereabouts of Mrs Gourley and they agreed to accompany him to Hotel Ontario to perform the difficult task of delivering the bad news to Pauline Gourley. When he arrived at the hotel Arcari summoned the

Night Manager who accompanied him to the Gourleys room. Pauline Gourley had descended into a deep sleep and completely non-responsive to the prodding of Joan Cagney in particular and it was decided to leave her to sleep off her hangover.

When she awoke hours later she was startled to find Joan and Bert by her bedside. "What are you doing here?" she exclaimed, "Where's John?" Looking round the room she caught sight of Captain Arcari, "He's not done anything stupid and got himself arrested has he?"

Captain Arcari smiled sympathetically before answering, "Mrs Gourley, I'm afraid we have some bad news for you. Your husband John has had a fatal accident. He slipped and lost his balance at the top of the Spanish Steps, which unfortunately resulted in a fractured skull and a broken neck. He did not suffer; his death was instantaneous."

Pauline stared around the occupants of the room before shock set in, her face cracking with anguish as the tears cascaded down her cheeks accompanied by loud wailing. Joan Cagney came forward, comforted her for what seemed an eternity while Luigi Arcari arranged for the hotel to contact a doctor in order to provide Pauline Gourley with a sedative.

The police contacted the British Embassy in Rome who took control in the aftermath of the unfortunate fatal accident on the Spanish Steps. They arranged for John Gourley's body to be brought back to Edinburgh accompanied by the recently widowed Pauline.

Several days later a report of John Gourley's sudden death arrived at Fettes Police headquarters, complete with CCTV evidence of the unfortunate accident, and was filed under 'Unsuspicious deaths.'

Michael Caldwell accepted the call from Seamus Carr which his secretary had put through to him.

"Morning Michael, I've just had some bad news from Tom Comerford. His friend John Gourley, who we interviewed about the Scotch Whisky industry last year has died suddenly in Rome."

"How did that happen Seamus?" responded Michael, knowing full well he had in fact ordered the assassination.

"Apparently, he was drunk, lost his footing on the Spanish Steps, and fell down the stairs breaking his neck."

"Oh dear, how horrible for his family. Thanks for letting me know Seamus. Sorry but I have a meeting shortly so I can't talk just now."

Michael didn't replace the telephone, instead dialled 'PK'. "Hello Patrick, Seamus Carr's just off the phone telling me that John Gourley's dead, but not the way we planned it. He had a bit of a freak accident losing his balance whilst drunk and falling, would you believe it, down the Spanish Steps. Divine guidance must be with us PK as this puts us in the clear and above suspicion."

PK smiled down the other end of the line, "Tough luck on our London friends. They've lost half their fee so we've saved ourselves £15,000 quid!"

Michael recognised the irony of the statement, "You're a hard man PK. See you soon to discuss where we go from here."

Michael Caldwell spent the next few months working on his plans to implement his attack on the Scotch whisky industry. Using the various members of his team to put in the final touches to all aspects of their strategy before they made their approach to the British government. Mhairi McClure and Colm set up a sophisticated system for distributing the ransom money using tax havens around the world from as far apart as Lichtenstein to Panama which currently handled their ill-gotten gains. Opening a harvest of small accounts, they would send them off around the world before exiting down an untraceable financial black hole.

Chapter 32

"Mr O'Reilly. I've got a Heime Dayan on the phone for you. He's calling from New York."

"Heime Dayan", questioned the silver-haired Gavin O'Reilly, "Sounds like a yid from New York. Don't normally deal with them, put him on and let me see what the Jews are pushing today. Hello Mr Dayan, Gavin O'Reilly speaking, what can I do for you today?"

"It's what I can do for you Mr O'Reilly." a soft yet high pitched voice replied. "Let me clarify some facts first. It was your son, who was murdered by British troops in May 1982. Am I correct in saying that at the time he was engaged to be married to Mhairi McClure?"

A shocked O'Reilly raised his voice, barking down the phone. "What's this got to do with you and what is it do with the New York Jewish community?"

The old Jewish negotiator continued in an unflappable tone, "Mr O'Reilly we gather intelligence from all regions of the earth and we have in our possession evidence regarding the death of your son, including the name of his killer."

A shudder ran through the veins of the Irish-American gang-leader, "But h-how did you get a hold of this information. I left no stone unturned in my effort to find the killers but my sources came up with a blank sheet. Tell me, who is the bastard responsible and I'll have him rubbed out!"

"Mr O'Reilly, you and I know that such information does not come free of charge so why don't we meet up and have more detailed discussions." Suggested Dayan "Okay where and when?" the frustrated O'Reilly asked.

"The Trump Towers, Tuesday afternoon 2.30'" replied Dayan before the phone clicked at his end.

A cool wind was blowing through Manhattan as Gavin O'Reilly alighted from his limousine outside Trump Towers surrounded by three minders with heavily-laden overcoats and his two business advisors Liam Peregrine and Larry Costello. Their progress was closely monitored by Mossad agents in different disguises placed strategically round the glass fronted building. The party proceeded to reception where the concierge informed them that Mr. Dayan was waiting for them in the Lewis Suite, named after Donald Trump's mother's birth-place. The Irish- American delegation were met at the door by two athletic looking young men wearing black suits which bulged under their armpits. They asked the O'Reilly delegation to raise their arms as they searched for firearms before opening the suite door.

Inside Dayan was waiting seated at a long polished oak table flanked by two colleagues. He rose immediately to greet his guests, "Mr O'Reilly many thanks for coming to New York to see us. Let me introduce my team, Ruben Silvester and Victor Krug who are both attached to Mossad in Tel Aviv where the information on your son first came to light."

The heavily built Silvester raised himself awkwardly out of his chair before shaking hands with Gavin O'Reilly followed by the slim close-cropped Victor Krug also greeting him.

Half-turning around Gavin responded "These guys are my business advisors Liam Peregrine and Larry Costello who are here to take the minutes of the meeting and make sure I don't agree to anything that would incriminate me in any way. Before we start, Larry will, with your permission, fleece the room for any cameras or recording equipment."

Dayan smiled and with a shake of the head raised his arms and said "Of course, we would do the same in your shoes."

The heavily-built Costello took a deep breath before forcing himself to his feet and placing a hand into his inside jacket pocket produced a small instrument which he held out in front of him as he traversed the room looking for surveillance material. The assembled company followed his progress round the room until Larry Costello signalled the all clear.

"Right let's get down to business Mr. O'Reilly. As I explained to you on the phone our intelligence people have unearthed information regarding the death of your son in Northern Ireland. Mossad prides itself in being one the most efficient intelligence agencies in the world and has only become so by setting high standards."

"So, what we do know is that British intelligence was concerned that your son Matt would rouse IRA sympathies by his visit and show the local Republican followers that the Irish in America were behind their aspirations for a United Ireland. A Special Forces commando squad from the SAS, based in Hereford, consisting of an officer and three marines were sent to successfully stop their advance by piercing the tyre of their Range Rover bringing their vehicle to an immediate halt. The occupants all got out of the Range Rover to be met by a hail of silencer bullets that left everyone dead except Matt."

Gavin O'Reilly blurted out. "If Matt didn't die immediately, how was he killed?"

Dayan intervened by raising his arm and calling for silence, "I know this must be difficult for you Mr. O'Reilly but is important that I convey my statement accurately. So, I would ask you to refrain from interrupting me."

Gavin nodded an apology before taking off his spectacles and wiping his eyes.

Dayan continued "What happened next is almost unbelievable. A young officer appeared from the foliage and taunted your son to the extent that he grabbed one of the guard's automatic pistols, but before he got anywhere near to firing it, Matt was gunned down by a marine. The officer re-acted badly as he knew there would be repercussions. After getting his men to despatch a few rounds using the Irish Republican weapons, to make it look like a self-defence situation, he then ordered them to 'stand down.' The officer then moved over and picking up the Glock automatic pistol, proceeded to assassinate his own three men. This was presumably to cover his tracks and to avoid ending his military career. He then radioed for assistance before using the Glock again to shoot himself in the hand which caused him to collapse in a heap. Within twenty minutes an army helicopter arrived taking the seven bodies on board. Shortly afterwards a Heavy Goods Vehicle was sent to the scene to take the Range Rover on board removing all signs off what had just taken place."

Liam Peregrine spoke first, "These Limey bastards are good at covering their tracks. What's the name of this officer who's responsible?"

"Before we get to that, there is no such thing as a free lunch and we would require some co-operation from your organisation by way of compensation." stated Dayan.

"Okay! What's the deal Mr. Dayan?" asked a frustrated Gavin O'Reilly.

"Currently" Dayan explained, "you collect donations from the Irish-American community which in turn you launder to the IRA in Dublin. They then use these funds to purchase weapons from Colonel Gadaffi in Libya who then sends the funds on to further the Palestinian cause in the Middle East. This is an annoyance that our government could do without and, although the money involved is miniscule, our duty is to cut off these funds at every opportunity."

His words created unease among the three gentlemen on the other side of the table. Larry Costello cleared his throat before responding angrily, "That's not on! The Provisionals rely on our generosity to fund the cause in the hope that some time down the line the British will give in and we shall get a United Ireland."

Ruben Sylvester smiled then replied, "Doesn't seem the Irish Government shares your pipe dream as they have signed the Good Friday Peace Agreement with Tony Blair's British regime."

Costello continued his aggressive line, "That won't stop the troops in the field continuing to wage war on the population in Northern Ireland who favour the Westminster government!"

Gavin O'Reilly didn't like his colleague's approach and intervened "Gentlemen, let's not get carried away. I am here today with the sole purpose of finding out the name of the man who killed my son. Mr. Dayan, your request will need ratification from ourselves after we have had time to discuss its consequences. If we agree to reduce our funding, how do you know that we will keep our word?"

"Good question Mr O'Reilly. Well, we could do one of two things - pass the information on to the British government who would do anything to cover their tracks to avoid an international incident, including arranging for your departure from this world."

"And the second option?"

"If we discovered that, having agreed to our terms, you were found to be contravening them by continuing to bankroll the IRA we would have the three of you assassinated." His words were met with gasps from the Bostonians who had all gone white with fright.

Dayan waved his arms to calm the meeting, "Now gentlemen, we don't want it to come to what I have just said. However, I should point out that Mossad has a reputation for succeeding with such assignments and the IRA are not seen as any real competition. I'll bring this meeting to a close now and ask you to get back to me within the week. If you decide against our proposal then no hard feelings, but you will not be able to avenge Matt's killers."

With that the Israelis rose from the table and shook hands with their somewhat shaken Irish-Americans visitors.

Five days later Gavin O'Reilly phoned Heime Dayan and agreed to his terms, namely, that his network would cease collections on the streets in the Eastern Seaboard for the IRA. Dayan reminded him of all the terms relating to his decision before releasing to him Colonel Colin Inglis's identity.

Gavin O'Reilly could not control his emotions, "This bastard Inglis is as good as dead, even MI5 won't stop me from getting him!"

When he put down the phone Dayan allowed himself a little smile as he a thought to himself, "Act 1 completed, now to get our people in London to consider starting negotiations with MI5 to discuss the subject of The 1972 Club'. The disc David Johnston had copied in Mhairi McClure's office will now prove to be a valuable weapon in these negotiations. No need to hurry, as I am sure a suitable opportunity will present itself before long. It always does in the scurrilous world of international espionage."

Chapter 33

OCTOBER 15th 1999

The Caledonian newspaper office in Edinburgh's North Bridge overlooking Princes Street received a brown envelope, delivered through the regular post addressed to the editor Hugh Ramsay marked 'Private and Confidential' It was opened by his personal assistant Cathy Gair. Inside, it contained a message made out of newspaper cuttings which read:

"Tell the Government that only a change to their policy on not paying compensation to terrorists will stop us wrecking a large part of the Scotch whisky industry unless they agree to our demand for £20m. Our plans are in place and the destruction can be activated at any time. When you have spoken to them, place a notice in your obituary column under the name Ismail Mohammed and we shall get back to you."

Cathy did not panic immediately as she was used to the paper receiving letters from cranks but there was something about this message which had been posted in London that worried her. Five minutes later she was standing in front of the diminutive, overweight Hugh Ramsay who was rubbing his eyes, ruffling his shock of red hair before replacing his spectacles.

"Morning Cathy, what midget gems have arrived in the post for me today? Not much news around so we could do with something to get our journalistic teeth into."

"Well Sir, this might suffice" replied Cathy, handing over the message.

Ramsay picked up the piece of paper and an eerie silence descended upon the room as he read its content. Finally, he spoke, "Do you think this is for real? 'Ismail Mohammed' would suggest that an Islamic fundamentalist group is behind it. I know there has been a lot of talk in the international press of a wealthy Saudi, Osama Bin Laden, declaring a war against the West. I am a little suspicious however about their request to place an obituary notice in the paper as Muslims bury their dead so quickly that they do not have any use for our services. Cathy, get the crime department to check out Ismail Mohammed, not that I think you will find out anything, and ask the Head of Crime to come and see me immediately."

The Head of Crime, Sandy Ross, knocked on the editor's door fifteen minutes later and sat down in one of the soft leather seats in front of his boss' desk and without hesitation uttered "Morning Hugh, if this is about the murder in Pumpherson we are no further forward so I apologise, but I am working on the report."

"That's good to know, but what do you make of this?" he asked passing over the note on his desk. Sandy picked it up and read it twice before replying.

"Well, it could be a crank but we are duty bound to contact the Home office to alert them. As for who is behind it, if it is for real, there are a number of organisations out there who would be attracted by the publicity, never mind the financial reward the success of this operation would bring. We're looking at a terrorist organisation of some sort, perhaps the Scottish Liberation Army but they would be reluctant to attack Scotland's national drink industry. More likely to be one of the Arab organisations, we know from bitter experience what they did at Lockerbie, but a demand for £20m is small beer when you are backed by Colonel Gadaffi. I would be more inclined to think that it is one of the smaller terrorist rogue cells whose funding has been cut off for one reason or another and they are going out on their own."

"Well summarised Sandy. Get a team together to find out all we can about what activities the terrorist industry is up to at present. I'll call the Home Secretary's office and suggest a Meeting a.s.a.p." Sandy hurriedly vacated his seat and left the Editor's office to brief his team on what he envisaged could be a major scoop.

Hugh Ramsay crossed his office and dialled the combination to his safe that was kept hidden behind the portrait of a previous owner of the paper. He took out a small notebook that contained very confidential telephone numbers, returned to his private phone and made a call to the Home Office. This was not a general call but one that linked directly to Armitage Brown, or 'AB' as he was known amongst the inner circle, and was in fact the Assistant Head Controller of MI5. After five rings AB spoke. "Hugh old boy, how are things in Bonnie Scotland, and to what do I owe this pleasure?"

"Morning Armitage, I received a message in my mail this morning from an unknown organisation, probably terrorists, when you hear what they have to say. They are demanding £20m from the Government or they will attack the Scotch Whisky industry."

There was a pregnant pause from AB before he gathered his thoughts and replied," Hugh read me out exactly what they have written."

Ramsay did as instructed and paused at the end, awaiting the reaction of the Home Office.

"Christ Hugh, this is cause for concern. The Scotch Whisky industry is one of the Treasury's biggest cash cows for tax revenues and apart from that has protected trade status. The Japanese and the Indian Governments have for a long time tried to push their own Whisky brands but this has been fought off in the courts successfully by the Scotch Whisky Association. However, if these nutters are genuine they could affect future spirit sales not to mention the reputational damage effect it would have on the whole British drinks industry. Do you have any suspicions as to who these people are? Has anybody ever heard of Ismail Mohammed?"

"No AB, but I have Sandy Ross, our head of Crime Reporting looking into it as we speak."

"Hugh, stop him immediately, this is far too sensitive an issue for your hacks to get into. Pull the whole team into your office and threaten them with the Official Secrets Act if you have to. I realise that you are after a scoop, and will promise that at all times we will keep you in the loop. I will have to report this to the PM's office. Do nothing until you hear from me. You can expect a visit from our forensic team who will want to analyse the message for any finger prints etc. Make sure that you can lay your hands on the envelope it arrived in."

"That might not be too easy as we shred all the envelopes every morning."

"Well cease that practice immediately!!" retorted AB, "Hugh I'll get back to you as soon as I can."

Hugh phoned Sandy Ross, "Sandy, bring your team to the office, there's been some further developments."

The Home Secretary took the Chair in the Cabinet office surrounded by all the experts in her department. Caroline Warrington had only been Home Secretary for a short time and was now facing her first major terrorist attack. With a brief touch of her hair which was increasingly showing streaks of grey, she opened the proceedings:

"Ladies and gentlemen, earlier today Armitage Brown received a telephone call from Hugh Ramsay the editor of the Caledonian newspaper in Edinburgh. He informed us that he was in receipt of an anonymous note made up of newspaper cuttings, demanding Her Majesty's Government pay £20m. pounds to avoid a devastating attack on the Scotch whisky industry. There is no evidence that is the work of some deranged individual and as no enemy group has come forward to claim responsibility for it we have to take the threat seriously. I will now open the meeting to any questions or suggestions you would like to make."

Ben Jackman, a senior civil servant with expertise in Middle East affairs was the first to speak, "This is a most unusual request from our military adversities as they have targeted an industry rather than densely populated area where they would receive the publicity these people usually crave."

The Minister agreed "Good point, Ben. AB do we know anything about this Ismail Mohammed?"

AB responded, "No nothing so far from our global agencies, who have contacted all their contacts but have drawn a blank."

The meeting continued for another hour with the Home Secretary being briefed by all the emergency services plus the military, who covered every contingency and explained how they would react to a threat of this nature without any leaks being given to the media in order not to spook the public.

"Thank you all for your contributions' summarised the Home Secretary, "AB will liaise with Editor Hugh Ramsay at the Caledonian and get him to place the obituary notice for Ismail Mohammed in Friday's edition of the paper."

"Why wait Four days until Friday Minister?" Brigadier Holton enquired on behalf of the army.

"'On Fridays, any self- respecting Muslim should be on his prayer mat. If we get a quick response then we'll know that we are unlikely to be dealing with Middle East terrorists."

Michael Caldwell scoured every edition of the Caledonian in the days following. He had personally posted the letter in London during a weekend break when he had taken his wife to London to see the musical 'Les Miserables' and the following evening a classical music concert at the Royal Albert Hall. The message had been meticulously prepared by Michael and he made certain there was nothing in it for forensics to exploit. On the Friday when the arranged obituary appeared Michael delayed responding, not because he wanted to, but his 'negotiator' Osman Helassie, a Libyan based in Cork, who supplied arms to the IRA, was at the Mosque. On the Saturday morning Michael briefed Osman on what his response to the death notice should be and when he should make contact.

Hugh Ramsay had instructed his P.A. that any call received from Ismail Mohammed was not to be put through to his office immediately in order to give the Intelligence Services who were camped in his office time to get their electronic analysis equipment connected. At 10.20 on the Monday morning a call came through from Ismail Mohammed.

The Libyan's soft voice began, "Ah, Mr Ramsay many thanks for your insert in Friday's edition of your paper. Please do not interrupt me as I only have a short time to get my information over to you and dispose of this mobile phone. I would suspect that this conversation is being recorded so you will have a record of our demands. We have over a considerable period of time placed a number of explosives in different whisky establishments around Scotland which we can detonate at any time we choose. We have decided upon these targets to avoid heavy casualties. In return, we want you to agree to our demand for £20m to be made available to us and distributed in a manner I will detail to you when I next call on Wednesday afternoon at 3.00p.m. your time. Goodbye."

The hollow sound of silence filled Hugh Ramsay's ears. The two intelligence technical officers repeatedly played the call over and over. One of them Mike Douglas was an expert in identifying dialects and within a short time he announced, "My money is on Mr Mohammed being Libyan, probably from the South of the country.'"

AB, who had set up a video link-up, did not doubt Mike's assessment but added the caveat, "This surprise me but I'll get our people in Tripoli on to it right away and find out what this is all about. Thanks boys - and you Hugh - for all your help. Fortunately, the Government has recently re-installed diplomatic relations with the Gadaffi regime after the Yvonne Fletcher and Lockerbie Bombing incidents have been partially resolved, so we should get an early feed-back."

Later that day Randolph Buxton met with the Libyan Foreign office and played them a recording of the message received from Ismail Mohammed. When the tape finished, Raki el Mademi, the Libyan deputy foreign minister clasped his hands together before confirming, "Your analysis of the caller's dialect is very accurate, Ismail Mohammed, I am always certain comes from the South. It is an area from which we have had some resistance to our policies so it does not altogether surprise me that someone from there is planning a major terrorist attack in the United Kingdom. I have alerted my surveillance teams throughout Libya and they have come up with a complete blank so far, but they have only been looking for a few hours."

"That's disappointing minister", Buxton sadly reflected "the Prime Minister was rather hoping that our recent resumption of co-operation between our governments would result in putting an end to this particular threat. Have you any further thoughts as to who might be behind this attack?"

Raki Mademi raised his hands in the air and twisted uncomfortably in his chair, "That is a difficult one

Ambassador Buxton, there are many groups throughout the Arab world who would take the opportunity to express their viewpoint in this manner against the West.

The obvious ones would be the Palestine Liberation Organisation, Iran or Sadam Hussain's Iraqi regime. If my surveillance teams come up with the same response as ourselves, it pains me to say it - and you never heard it from me, I would talk to the Israelis."

The meeting terminated and Randolph waited until he was in his car before phoning Armitage Brown and giving him the sombre news. "That's too bad Buxton. Give the Libyans forty-eight hours to respond. In the meantime, I'll speak to my counterpart at Mossad in Tel Aviv."
Chapter 34

Benny Vinestock was surprised to get the call from AB. They had known each other very well when they were based in Berlin during the Cold War. Then AB spent his time tackling the Russian's secret codes while Benny busied himself with searching out Nazi war criminals.

"Hello AB, this is indeed a great surprise or should I say honour to address the Head of MI5' he added sarcastically, 'what can the people of Israel do for the British Government."

"Glad to see your bullshit is still as thick as ever, and by the way it is Assistant Head" joked AB, 'Well, we have a situation that has arisen which we are struggling to resolve. If you have a few minutes I'll explain."

"Please do, I like a good mystery."

AB outlined events to date and how his department were unable to uncover the source of the terrorist threat to the U.K. When he finished Benny smiled before resuming the conversation. "You're hoping that we can shed some light on this group who are almost certainly enemies of the State of Israel! I don't know if we can, but if we could, what is in it for us? Armitage, the Jew boy in me always comes out and so I'd be looking to cut a deal that would enhance my Government's cause."

"Benny, my Government is taking this threat seriously so there could be some exchanges we could make that might satisfy your masters. We can discuss this when you come up with information that assists our enquiries."

"Armitage leave it with me. It will take a few days to get back to you but Tel Aviv are always happy to keep good relations with the British Government so we'll leave no stone unturned."

"Thanks Benny. Speak to you soon."

AB replaced his phone despondently. So far, he was not getting anywhere in his efforts to identify Ismail Mohammed. Picking up the phone again he asked his PA Carol Wardrop to put in a call to the Scottish Secretary of State Jack Lindsay. Within minutes Lindsay was on the phone.

Using his polite West of Scotland accent Lindsay opened the conversation, "Mr Brown, Jack Lindsay here, how can I help you? It is not every day that we junior ministers get to speak to the controllers of MI5."

Armitage ignored reciprocating any pleasantries but launched straight into the problem that was currently frustrating him, "Thanks Mr Lindsay for getting back to me so promptly. I'll get right to the point. Through their normal mail last week, the Caledonian newspaper received a note demanding us, the Government that is, pay a ransom of £20m or run the risk of significant damage to Scotch whisky installations spread throughout your country."

"Bloody Hell, who are these people!"

"That's the dilemma MI5 have. We don't know who they are, although we have put out a search globally which to date has proved negative. This matter is being treated as 'Top Secret'. The editor at the Caledonian and his staff, have already signed the Official Secrets Act. However, as this terrorist attack is potentially going to be carried out on your patch I want you to call a top priority briefing meeting of all Area Chief Constables and Fire Chiefs. I want a special team from each area division to troll through their records looking for any incidents that could in anyway be connected to the Whisky trade. We have to keep this threat under wraps so do not alert the Scotch Whisky Association at this stage. I will be your direct contact at MI5, but should I be unavailable ask for Carlton Montague, my assistant"'

"Sounds I like a name from a John Le Carre novel," an amused Jack Lindsay replied.

"Yes, and before you ask, his background is Eton and Cambridge University. Get back to me once you have briefed your top cops Mr. Lindsay. Good day." Chapter 35

Jack Lindsay contacted The Police Training College at Tulliallan, spoke to Principal Robert Watson and asked him to co-ordinate a meeting of all the Area Chief Constables plus their Fire Service and Ambulance counterparts, on the misconception that there were changing procedures for emergency services in Scotland emanating out of a directive from Westminster. Tulliallan was a suitable venue as it was very central but more importantly a gathering of emergency service leaders meeting there was normal, and would not attract the media. Watson responded to the urgency of the request and two days later Jack Lindsay and his PPS made their way to Clackmannanshire to rendezvous with the Police Chiefs.

After passing through the strict security barrier the Scottish secretary's limousine, flanked by two police motorcyclists, drove up the long driveway bordered by large oak trees to the main house where they were greeted by the Chief Constable of the college, Alex Bunyan. The party proceeded to a large private lecture room, where tea and coffee was served to the assembled civil protectors. After fifteen minutes, everyone was summoned to take their places around the table where nameplates and the agenda for today's meeting were already in place on its shiny surface.

A solemn faced Jack Lindsay commenced the proceedings:

"Good morning, ladies and gentlemen, many thanks for coming together at such short notice. I am aware that you are all under pressure to ensure the protection of public safety which is of utmost importance, so I'll get straight to the point of why you are here. The brief you received from my office intimated that the purpose of the meeting as 'to discuss changes in procedures issued by Central Government', but you can ignore that." His words were met with bewilderment by the assembled audience. "Last week Hugh Ramsay, the editor of the Caledonian, received a message in his mail from a terrorist organisation, a copy of which you have in front of you, threatening to destroy parts of the whisky trade if they do not receive a ransom of £20m.' Lindsay's last few words brought gasps from the Police Chiefs.

Jack Lindsay continued, "MI5 have been given the task of leading the investigation to identify the group responsible but so far they have nothing concrete to report. I have been asked to convene this meeting and have a brainstorming session with yourselves in the hope that we can uncover something relevant to find out who these terrorists are. The problem we have is that so far, we have had little to go on, Ismail Mohammed, name of the go-between, would suggest that we are dealing with a Middle East group, although no one has come forward to claim responsibility.

The problem is that the whisky industry is so fragmented geographically with distilleries spread from the Lothians, through the Central Region, to the West of Scotland and finally the Highlands and Islands. So, we don't know where the threat will come from. All your constabularies could be affected. I'll up the meeting now for general discussion and try to answer any questions you may have."

Mutterings filled the room before the first contribution came from Rae Donaldson, Central Regions' Chief of

Police. Puffing his cheeks out as if wondering where to start he said, "Sir this is not an easy one for any of us. Just up the road from here is one of the biggest grain distilleries in Scotland at Castlebridge, but more importantly the bonded warehouses at Alva and Hillfoots between them hold a large percentage of the whisky stocks in Scotland. We do monitor their boundaries closely on a daily basis but anything that goes on internally comes under the auspices of the Customs and Excise. The problem we have is that we don't know if they will infiltrate my side of the business or go for one of the big blending houses that may be easier to access.'

Jack Lindsay nodded in agreement, 'Yes, Clackmannanshire is a worry. The only thing going for it is that it is sparsely populated and could be evacuated quickly should it be necessary to do so. George, how do you see things in Fife?' asked the meeting Chairman turning to George McLeish, Fife's Chief of Police.

The balding McLeish looked round the room before replying, "My fear is the Lundin bottling hall which feeds off bonded warehouses the size of several football pitches. There are hundreds of workers involved, badge marketing several famous brands for the global whisky market. If it turns out that my area is the target it will be a major logistical task to clear the surrounding area. We are sitting here lacking in data so can I suggest that we shift the discussion on and try to co-ordinate where we go from here. From what it states in this message it appears that they are confident of their ability to infiltrate the whisky industry but they don't give us a clue as to how they are going to do it. If some nutter has

211

access to a rocket launcher, for instance, then the consequences could be catastrophic."

Cyril Sym, Strathclyde's top cop intervened, "Minister has there been any policy change by No. 10 regarding paying ransom demands?"

"No!' retorted Jack Lindsay, 'The PM will not hear of it. He does not want to start an avalanche of demands from every corner of the terrorist world. Now I have to hear what the rest of your colleagues have to contribute. It is very much a WHO? WHAT? WHERE? WHEN? HOW? And I want to get everybody's thoughts on this one."

For the next hour, the Fire and Police Chiefs gave an outline of where the threat could emanate. Some described how a major explosion could affect other large industrial plants or hospitals as well as the densely populated cities like Edinburgh and Glasgow.

Jack Lindsay called the meeting to order. "Ladies and Gentlemen, I appreciate your input. Ambrose Brown at MI5 has asked that you each organise teams made up of your best investigators and search your records for incidents that are related to the whisky industry in any way. This operation will have the code name 'Operation Large Scotch', O.L.S. to all of you, and has been given the highest security alert. You and your teams will all have to sign the Official Secrets Act. All findings uncovered must be sent directly to my office where they will be coordinated before being passed to MI5.

My contact details are enclosed in your dossiers. Meeting is now closed. Good Luck and a safe journey home."

The officers rose from the table with serious expressions on their faces and were all engaged in deep thought as they bade farewell to their contemporaries.

As his driver traversed the Kincardine Bridge Superintendent Peter Anderson reached for his phone and made a call to Lothian & Borders headquarters in Edinburgh. It took eight rings before a female voice answered but then wished she hadn't when Anderson shouted down the phone "Where the hell have you been? I called using my special number so I don't expect to be kept waiting. Tell Sylvia Dalrymple, your boss, to come and see me first thing in the morning! Now without delay put me on to Chief inspector Grant McKirdy."

All across Scotland the area police forces were instructed to look for anything which connected criminals to the whisky trade. No stone was left unturned and soon data emerged which included everything from parking fines to
breaches of the peace following drunken brawls in local hostelries.

Chapter 36

The day after the Tulliallan Conference, Superintendent Anderson met with D. I. Grant Mckirdy, D.S. Neil Lamont and D.C. Margaret Wright. Mckirdy explained everything that had happened to date concerning 'Operation Large Scotch' (now referred to as 'O.L.S.') and asked them to handle the enquiry on behalf of Lothian & Borders Police and due to the sensitive nature of the terrorist threat, only use other staff when necessary.

"Can you think of anything that immediately springs to mind with links to the whisky trade?" asked Anderson more in hope than anything else.

Neil Lamont surprised the other three by re-acting quickly to the question. "Yes, I can, just over a year ago in September 1998 there was the murder of Allan Phair in Edinburgh. He was a University professor who was an advisor to the whisky trade. We have never solved that murder, but at the time we thought it had the hallmark of a contract killing."

"Brilliant Neil. Well remembered" congratulated D.I. McKirdy, "Let's get out all the papers on that one and see where it takes us."

"Back to the Edinburgh University Swingers Club!" joked Margaret Wright. A remark not appreciated by Superintendent Anderson who was not familiar with the details of the Phair Murder Case.

Breaking the pregnant pause Lamont continued, "Well one things for certain, we can score Mhairi McClure off our list, considering she accused Allan Phair of raping her, which is something his widow will not want to hear."

Three days later at the L & B headquarters at Fettes 'The O.L.S.' team re-convened to discuss their progress but nothing obvious had been recovered. However, D.C. Wright surprised her colleagues by including in her surveillance, accidental deaths in Lothian & Borders, which brought to the fore the name of John Gourley. Wright gave a brief outline to the others, "John Gourley was on holiday in Rome when he slipped and fell down the Spanish Steps breaking his neck and dying instantly. Gourley worked at the Scotia distillery here in Edinburgh as a labourer in the spirit store where they fill the whisky casks."

Superintendent Anderson intervened, "But how would that connect him to a Middle East terrorist organisation?"

"Well Sir, Gourley was Irish and it was on a trip home to Strathane that a friend bought him a raffle ticket, the first prize in which was a short break in Rome with £500 spending money."

"What was the name of the club in Strathane?" demanded Anderson.

"The Republican Club," replied D.C. Wright.

"Good thinking Margaret!" D.I. McKirdy exclaimed "let's delve further into your lead. We shall have to see if there were any photos in the Italian press regarding the accident, possibly taken by tourists at the time or CCTV. I have been to the Spanish Steps and it is normally louping with tourists."

'I'll get on to it right away Sir.'

DC Wright ploughed through all the media coverage of John Gourley's accident including photographs taken by tourists and CCTV camera evidence gathered by the Italian police. She decided to circulate them to all the police forces in the UK in case someone could recognise a witness who might be worth interviewing regarding the accident. She was more than a little surprised when Inspector Jack Birch of the Met phoned her the day after her message was sent out.

"D.C. Wright, Jack Birch at the Met here. It's was about the photographs you sent down. It may be nothing but one of my men recognised two of the bystanders, who are known hit-men, and we hardly think they are the type who would be taking in Roman culture. We are going to bring them in for questioning today and will inform you of the outcome."

"Great sir, I am not at liberty to tell you about the crime we are investigating - You would have to get your Commissioner to phone Superintendent Anderson of L & B for that. However, in the course of your interrogation ask if they have any dealings with Irish criminals." "Okay Miss Wright I'll keep that in mind."

Mike Turnbull and Peter Hone were drinking in the Iron Horse pub In Bermondsey when a squad of plain clothes cops entered the pub from doors on either side of the hostelry, surrounded them and escorted them to cars outside. The cavalcade set off a speed for New Scotland Yard.

Jack Birch and detective Barrie Rostron entered the 'Interrogation Room 2' where Turnbull and Hone were sitting at a desk, in the company of two burly police officers. Both men were smaller than Birch had expected although they were both very fit-looking as you would expect from former SAS troopers. "Afternoon gentlemen, you must be wondering why we are wasting your time today just when you were enjoying a drink in the Iron Horse."

"You know us, Mr Birch we are always happy to help the Met out in any way we can." Turnbull said sarcastically.

"Okay Turnbull, don't get ahead of yourself. You might be grateful of our assistance before today is out." Birch opened the folder in front of him and took out the photos supplied by Lothian & Borders. "Now can I ask you how you two happened to be in Rome witnessing a fatal accident on the Spanish Steps?"

Birch placed the evidence in front of Turnbull and Hone who stared in disbelief that they had appeared in an Italian national newspaper, as experienced assassins never normally leave anything to chance. "Well gents what's your explanation?" asked Birch.

The two looked at each other for a moment before Hone replied, "We just went sight- seeing for a few days, taking our motorbikes for a run and having a night out with the Cosa Nostra." he smirked.

"Oh, that's not what the intelligence are saying boys. We understand you were there representing the IRA" Birch lied to the startled duo.

"We haven't done anything illegal!" Turnbull retorted.

217

"Nobody said you had gentlemen but if you value your freedom for the next forty-eight hours and possibly beyond, I suggest you start singing some of that Italian Opera to us. Who asked you to go to Rome and for what purpose?"

"Mr Birch can we have a moment in private before answering that question?"

"Okay Turnbull, we'll go and have a fag."

On the closure of the door Turnbull and Hone went into deep discussion for ten minutes then asked one of their guards to get the detectives to return.

"Mr Birch as we said you have our word that we did nothing illegal when we were in Rome. You can't hold us for something we didn't do but to help your enquiries I would speak to an Irishman called Pat Kearney or 'PK' as he's known."

D.I. Birch smiled across the table "'Thank you for your co-operation gentlemen. We'll leave it at that for now."

Birch wasted no time in getting his report up North to D.C. Wright who convened another meeting with her colleagues.

"The Met have interviewed Mike Turnbull and Peter Hone who they recognised from the photographs I circulated. They are suspected of being professional hit men, but to date have not left the Met with enough evidence to get a conviction. At the interview, they started off by telling D.I. Birch that they had gone for a motorcycle holiday to Europe. When they were pressurised by D.I. Birch and D.S. Rostron, who informed them that they had information connecting them to Irish

218

terrorists, they turned Queen's evidence and named an Irishman Patrick Kearney as someone we should interview."

Superintendent Anderson was very impressed with the results and relieved to be dealing with the IRA of whom his force had some experience.

Sergeant Lamont then had his turn to update the team on his progress and how he had taken a leaf out of D.C. Wright's book.

"Before I get into my report, Margaret, that's very interesting what you said about the two suspects at the Met taking their motorcycles on a long trip. When we were investigating Allan Phair's murder a member of the public remembered a motorcycle with a pillion rider going at speed away from the scene of the crime. It might be worth you calling D.I. Birch back and get him to have a close look at their motorbikes for forensic evidence. Also interview them as to their whereabouts in September 1998."

"Thanks for that Neil, I'll get on to it right away."

Neil was feeling very pleased with himself now and started his update;

"I started broadening the unsolved murder field and discovered the case of David Johnson who was run over in Belfast in 1988 for no apparent reason. The RUC supplied footage of the funeral and I was surprised that it featured none other than Mhairi McClure offering condolences to the late David's son John. On making enquiries it transpires that Mhairi McClure was one of the last people to see David Johnson alive, when he called at her office to fix her computer. Looking into Mhairi McClure's CV, I realised she was the fiancée of Matt O'Reilly, a Boston based IRA sympathiser, who was shot in 1982 as he was about to start campaigning in Northern Ireland. When you throw the Allan Phair unsolved murder into the pot, it would appear that Miss McClure is a very dangerous lady to know. Last Friday she left her office in Belfast and caught a plane to London but has not been seen since."

"You really have been busy Neil," D.I. McKirdy acknowledged, "I hope she is not working as a lone wolf bearing in mind her expertise in the I.T. field."

Two days later at the Met in London D.S. Rostron popped his head round D.I. Birch's office door, "Sir, Turnbull and Hone have arrived."

"Good, show them into our interrogation room and I will be right with you."

Five minutes later Jack Birch sat down opposite Mike Turnbull and Peter Hone. "Morning Gentlemen, sorry to bring you back in, but we just wanted to clarify something in your statement. Last time you were here you mentioned going across to Europe on your motorcycles. That's quite a trip, are you both keen motorbike riders?"

They looked at each other before answering,

"Yes" replied Turnbull, "but what has this to do with our last visit here?"

D.S. Rostron ignored the question and continued, "To take a trip like that you must have powerful bikes."

Hone responded, "Mike and I both have Honda CBR Firebirds 918cc that we bought new in a deal we did with Bermondsey Bikes in Albert Road. That was back in July 1998 but we can let you see all the paperwork for them."

D.I. Birch stirred in his chair, "Now that's interesting. Have either of you ever been to Edinburgh, say in September 1998? Because Lothian & Border Police have an unsolved murder of Professor Allan Phair they are still investigating. A member of the public reported seeing a motorbike speeding through an area close to the crime scene with a pillion rider on the back. Does that bring back any memories gentlemen?"

"We accept that you did not have anything to do with the unfortunate Mr Gourley falling down the Spanish Steps in Rome. However, do you not think it is very coincidental that the two corpses we are discussing are both from Edinburgh, both were employed in the Scotch Whisky industry in one shape or form? To cap it all they have both recently, like yourselves, made contacts with characters based in Northern Ireland!"

"No comment" was heard simultaneous from the accused.

"Very well, we are detaining you for further enquiries and we shall require to have the motorcycles brought in to be examined by our forensic teams. Our colleagues in Edinburgh will want you to account for your movements at the time. Does that help loosen your tongues?"

"No comment, but we require a solicitor," replied a very uneasy Peter Hone. Jack Birch leaned across the table.

"He won't do you pair any good. Guilt is written all over your faces. Your role in life has always been to eliminate chosen targets which you have probably done successfully, but when faced with interrogation you are out of your league, so look forward to a long stay in prison."

Looking up he continued, "Officer, get Mike Turnbull and Peter Hone beds for the night."

Chapter 37

Ismail Mohammed interrupted the Editor's Monday
Meeting at the Caledonian with his call to Hugh Ramsay.
The editor cleared the room before answering. The caller
began, "Mr Ramsay, once more I will be brief. There has
been no response from the Government to our demands
so by way of demonstrating that we are serious we
intend to explode our first bomb. The one we have
chosen is cask No. 9612 filled at the Scotia Distillery,
which now lies in a bond in Kinnoull Street Perth. Unless
you want to see parts of Perth being destroyed you have
forty-eight hours to have it neutered or we shall set it off
by remote control devastating large parts of the Fair
City." At that the phone went dead.

MI5 was alerted immediately and AB wasted no time in
contacting the bomb disposal squad housed at
Craigiehall on the western outskirts of Edinburgh.
Captain David Paton listened as AB briefed him on the
terrorist threat before responding. "Mr Brown, I will get
my team together without delay and will get the RAF to
helicopter our equipment up to Perth. This will be an
intricate operation as we will have to get the bond
owners to give us the exact location of Cask 9612 and
see if we can transport it to the nearest safe location to
carry out a controlled explosion."

AB replied, "Leave the logistics to us. I will call the bond
owner's offices in Perth and report back to you by the
time your men are in place." "Thank you, Sir. Speak to
you later."

Kinnoull Street was a small bond situated near the centre of Perth surrounded by a number of commercial offices. Decisions would have to be made regarding clearing the population to a safe distance from the potential bomb threat. AB thought this could prove tricky as the Government did not want to spook the public and cause widespread panic.

By the time the Bomb Squad touched down on North Inch Golf Course near the River Tay the Warehouseman, Alistair Dickson, who had not been briefed why barrel 9612 was being removed, had cleared the way for the bomb squad to gain access. Captain Paton's team of four, including himself, made their way into the bond and using sophisticated technology sought to identify the whereabouts of an explosive device. An X-ray of the barrel revealed the small package of Semtex at the base of the barrel.

"There's definitely something there, Sir," Corporal Ireland informed his commanding officer. "We shall have to be careful how we move it. Depending how it has been wired up, any effort to remove it by rolling it out of the bond to safety could trigger it off. I would suggest we carefully lift it on to a fork-lift and take it to a safe place to carry out a controlled destruction of its contents." Captain Paton rubbed his chin before replying, "Is there any way we could open it up to see in more detail what we are dealing with?"

"Not easy Sir. We are dealing with a potentially highly flammable liquid and if it goes off suddenly that will be the end of us all. We also have to aware that there could be enemies in the vicinity who could implement the remote-control procedure."

"Point taken. I think the easiest way to move this would be to make use of the helicopter and take that cask over to the Queens Barracks at Dunkeld where we can carry out the controlled bang. Better alert the local radio station - after we do it to save further panic.'

The public were cleared from the area within a twohundred-yard radius of Kinnoull Street under the pretext that the bond owners were making an advert. The helicopter took minutes to secure a grasp around the barrel, lift it clear of the town and fly on a route along the River Tay before transporting it north to its final destination at the Queens Barracks. Other members of the bomb squad had set up a bomb-proof shelter near the barracks and carried out the safe disposal of Cask 9612.

Scottish Bomber Command filmed the controlled explosion and kept AB constantly informed about events in Perth, which if nothing else confirmed that the terrorist threat was a very real one.

Chapter 38

It was late in the day when Benny Vinestock telephoned AB. "Evening Armitage how are things in London?"

"Bloody awful" blurted out AB.

"Well, I have some news that will make your day."

"Don't tell me that you have signed a peace treaty with the PLO."

"Easy Armitage, or I will put down the phone."
threatened Benny jocularly.

"Sorry Benny, this terrorist threat is getting to me,"
apologised the MI5 boss, "Please continue."

"My colleagues here at Mossad have looked through our
records and may have uncovered the cell that is
bothering you at present. It's an interesting story and
one that you may not entirely like. One of our agents
reported some ten years ago about a group calling
themselves the 1972 Club, based in Northern Ireland.
They were supporting the republican cause but, at the
same time, filling their pockets through controlling their
communities by way of protection rackets and drug
trafficking. I am not at liberty to say who supplied this
data but Mossad checked it out and are satisfied it is
genuine."

"So why haven't we heard about this before?" shouted
AB down the phone, not able to contain his anger.
"Silence Armitage", answered Vinestock, "If you think
that's bad, wait until you hear the rest of the story. By
the way, Mossad holds all sorts of information that we
use as insurance to secure 'favours' from other
governments as and when we require them. But back to
the case in hand, you will recall that back in 1982 you
sent a hit squad of SAS to Northern Ireland with the sole
purpose of frightening an American, Matt O'Reilly who
had come to canvas republican causes in the province.
Not everything went to plan and O'Reilly was killed.
What you don't know is that the three SAS soldiers killed
were gunned down by a Lieutenant Colin Inglis using one
of the IRA guns."

"'Benny that's preposterous, Inglis, Colonel Inglis as he is now, is a first-class officer who works for me to this day! I cannot accept such a charge being made against a trusted member of my team!"

"You can think what you like Armitage, but Inglis was seen in London by the same witness who supplied the info on the 1972 Club. It is highly unlikely a case of mistaken identity, when Inglis is missing two fingers of his right hand!

I appreciate this opens up a can of worms for you that will develop into a major incident should the media get a hold of the story. The families of the dead soldiers will be screaming for a public enquiry and the legal profession will be licking their lips like hyenas as they scavenge for legal fees. However, another section of Mossad has passed information to the O'Reilly family regarding Colin Inglis, so they will be placing a contract out on him. That could rid you of a delicate problem." the Israeli spy chief concluded.

Silence, then AB replied "Christ, Benny you have not made it easy for me. I'll need time to think about this. In the meantime, can you supply us with a list of the senior commanders at the 1972 Club?"

"My staff in Jerusalem will deliver it to your embassy there. In return, Armitage, the next time we need clearance on any new UK manufactured weapons we will not expect any resistance to their availability by interfering Muslim sympathisers in your House of Commons."

"Okay, Benny, I'll have your request passed on to Customs & Excise. Goodnight and thanks for the headache."

AB flicked the switch on his intercom, "Carlton, can you bring me through Colin Inglis's file?" "Right away Sir," replied his P.A.

AB examined the Inglis file in detail and the ill-fated 1982 attack in Northern Ireland in particular which led him to call Major George Gilzean, who had now retired to the Lake District. 'Afternoon George, sorry to break up your quiet life in Ullswater, but a little problem has emerged and I would like your slant on it. Back in 1982, you had cause to visit Lieutenant Colin Inglis, now Colonel Inglis, in hospital in Birmingham following a shooting incident

in Northern Ireland. I know that it is a long time ago but did you have any concerns about the patient at the time.'

Gilzean hesitated before speaking, "I'm just trying to think Mr Armitage... Now if I recall correctly, the only thing I thought was incorrect is that when Inglis contacted HQ he said he had been shot in the arm but in actual fact he had been hit in the hand resulting in the loss of two fingers. Seemed to me very inaccurate, and not the sort of thing one would get wrong."

'Unless he phoned in before he fired the shots at himself', thought the cynical spy chief to himself.

"Well thanks for your information Major, I'll let you get back to your bird-watching. Goodbye and thanks."
Chapter 39

"Mhairi, how are you? Long time since we last spoke. Gavin O'Reilly here. I'm coming across to London next week and wondered if we could meet up. The purpose of my visit concerns Matt and I think you should be there. I don't want to say anymore on the phone. Are you free on that weekend?"

"Gavin, how nice to hear from you. Yes, I can make it across to London at the weekend as it does not interfere with my university work. Will your wife be accompanying you Gavin?"

"No, it's business. Look give me your address and I'll get my travel agents to book airfares and a decent hotel in London. I want to be as discreet as possible so I will book a suite with adjoining rooms and book you in as Mrs O'Reilly. Don't be alarmed by that and again I will explain it all to you when we meet."

Mhairi furnished O'Reilly with her details.

"Fine, it's a date, see you next weekend."

The following Friday afternoon Mhairi McClure went straight from the university to Belfast airport and caught a British Airways flight to London. She then took a taxi to the Lancaster Hotel. Gavin O'Reilly had arrived earlier in the day and had gone out again but he had left a message for Mhairi to meet him at a restaurant in Kensington at 8 o'clock. This gave Mhairi time to have a bath and prepare herself for what would be an unforgettable evening.

Wearing a navy blue tight fitting cocktail dress Mhairi entered the Goodnight Restaurant and asked the head waiter to show her to Mr O'Reilly's table which was on the first floor overlooking the main dining room. Gavin smiled when he saw Mhairi approaching and stood up to greet her.

"Mhairi McClure! You look great. I am the envy of all the other diners here tonight, he boasted in a loud voice which attracted the attention of some of the clientele, causing Mhairi some embarrassment.

Gavin had aged well, although Mhairi was aware of a walking stick next to his seat. After ordering drinks and giving their waiter their orders, Gavin began to speak about the purpose of his visit. "Mhairi, it is now seventeen years since Matt was assassinated in Northern Ireland and I left no stone unturned in trying to find his killers but to no avail. The British establishment pulled ranks and my enquiries hit a brick wall. However, I recently had a visit from a very unusual source, the Israeli security services Mossad. They have released the name of Matt's killer to me."

Mhairi could not contain herself, "How did they manage that and who are these scoundrels who ruined both our lives!"

Gavin continued, "Let me tell you what I know then we can concentrate on the one man responsible." O'Reilly then related the whole sordid tale to Mhairi who listened intently until he finished.

"Gavin this is extraordinary, and you are satisfied that the information is accurate? If you give me the name of the witness I'll have him picked up and interrogated."

"Sorry Mhairi, the Israelis refused to reveal their source but I have made enquiries independently and am satisfied that the responsible officer is Colonel Colin Inglis."

"So where is he based now? And what do you intend to do about him?" an angry Mhairi enquired.

"I have been in London for a few days with members of my security team and we have been observing Inglis's movements. He is a senior MI5 officer who subconsciously watches what is going on around him so he is not easy to surprise. He is a very keen horse racing fan and is going to a race meeting at Kempton Park this weekend and will not be expecting to meet an attractive Irish Horse owner." Gavin concluded with a smile.

"What do you intend to do to him?"

"Lure him to a quiet spot where my team will arrange to abduct him and bring him to me, then my intention is to do to him what he did to Matt a long time ago - to kill the Bastard! To answer your first question the reason I chose this restaurant, and this particular table is that if you look down below to the large table of diners making the most noise, the gentlemen in the bright sports coat. He is Colonel Colin Inglis."

Mhairi stared down at the diners and had difficulty resisting going down the stairs to the dining room and scratching the killer's eyes out. Gavin had anticipated her reaction and held her wrist while at the same time offering her a handkerchief to mop up the tears that welled up from her green eyes.

"Let it be, Mhairi. All in our own good time!"

When they got back to the hotel Gavin introduced Mhairi to his bodyguards Conrad and Padraig over a drink in his suite. 'Right guys what have you observed today regarding Colonel Inglis?'

Conrad Dunne, the younger of the two, spoke first, "The colonel is a creature of habit and we think the best time for us to confront him is first thing in the morning when he takes his dog across to the park. Yesterday we thought of abducting him during the race meeting at Kempton Park on Saturday but they are expecting a large crowd which would make it very difficult for us. Sunday morning will be quieter for the plan of attack we have in mind."

Mhairi responded to the suggestion, "So how are you going to go about it? I would like to be involved as that bastard ruined my life!"

"Don't worry Mhairi, you'll have a ringside seat as I'll just explain to you." declared Conrad Dunne.

Chapter 40

At seven o'clock on Sunday morning Elgin Square Garden was host to some litter left over from the revelry of the night before plus a few joggers. Colin Inglis, wearing a green wax jacket and a brown trilby hat, entered and let his golden retriever Candy off the lead. After walking for a few minutes, he was passed by an attractive runner in a blue Lycra tracksuit who only travelled another one hundred and fifty yards before coming to an abrupt halt clasping her hamstring and hobbling to a nearby bench.

Two runners coming in the opposite direction stopped to assist her as Inglis approached. One addressed the Colonel in an American accent, "Excuse me Sir, do you have a mobile phone? This lady is going to need some medical attention."

"Yes" replied by the Colonel reaching into his inside pocket and coming closer to the bench. Making what was his last final movement, he passed the phone to the distressed lady. The two assassins wasted no time. Conrad, who had been clapping the dog, slid his fingers under the hound's collar and sunk a needle into its neck, causing it to give out a sharp yelp before it lost consciousness. Padraig assisted by his colleague grabbed the unsuspecting security chief and held him in an armlock long enough for Mhairi to produce a cyanide syringe from her water bottle that she plunged into his neck as she screamed into his ear "And that's for Matt O'Reilly, the fiancée you deprived me of!!"

The three killers positioned the corpse on the bench as though he were asleep with his faithful companion, still on a lead resting peacefully at his feet. Using his gloved hand Conrad stuck Inglis's phone in one of the dead man's pockets. The three of them jogged off, as though nothing had happened, towards a car waiting a few hundred yards away at one of the entrances to the park. The assassination had taken less than a minute to complete.

Chapter 41

The information given by Mossad was passed to all the senior officers from the secret service, the army and the emergency services, who were positioned round the table at the MI5 headquarters in Whitehall.

AB spoke first, "Gentlemen the file in front of you was supplied to us from the Israeli secret service Mossad a few days ago. Since then my staff have put together dossiers on the members of The 1972 Club which you will see has thrown up some very unlikely terrorist candidates. We have been searching for suspects who have threatened to wreck large parts of the Scotch Whisky industry unless they are paid a ransom of £20m. To date our contact has been an 'Ismail Mohammed' but we suspect he may be a decoy so we have decided to organise a raid on the leaders of the 1972 Club, sooner rather than later, and that is what we have to organise today."

Brigadier Tate, a veteran of the Irish troubles spoke up immediately, "Surprise is an understatement. I knew Michael Caldwell during my time in Northern Ireland when he was a senior lecturer at Queens University and he was never suspected as being an IRA sympathiser. The only other leading figure I recognise is Pat Kearney, who is a real nasty piece of work with whom we should have dealt with years ago but it was felt that his presence was more valuable controlling the hotheads in his district."

"Thanks for that Brigadier, good to know that you are acquainted with our suspects. Now how do you think we

234

should go about planning to meet up with them in person?"

"Surprise is nearly always our best weapon so I think we should schedule a major attack simultaneously on all the senior members of the 1972 Club. Sunday mornings are usually best as the roads are quieter and many people are sound asleep having over imbibed the night before."

"Good" concurred AB, "Please get all the logistics of the attack in place for implementation next Sunday morning at 0500 hours. Keep me informed of your progress and any contingencies that could affect the success of our plan."

"Do we have a name for the operation?" enquired the Brigadier.

"Stick with Operation Large Scotch", replied AB, "we will all be in need of a large Scotch when this is over!"

On a very chilly November Sunday morning fleets of unmarked cars made their way through Northern Ireland and positioned themselves for a five o'clock simultaneous assault on six rather different properties. All the commanders, who each had a team of a dozen SAS soldiers under their command, were linked to headquarters and nervously awaited the signal to attack.

Michael Caldwell's property was the most demanding target since he lived in a large house, set in its own grounds, out in the country. The security forces had it ring-fenced and were moving in on their target by fourfifty ready for the signal to attack. What they had not allowed for was the Caldwell's dog who started barking and woke his master up. Michael Caldwell jumped out of bed and looked out the window into the darkness but could see no sound of intruders. However, Luke continued to snarl and bark vociferously at the front door. Michael opened the door just enough for the dog to exit the house, closed it quickly and went to the window to watch the animal's progress. The collie used his sheepdog instincts and headed towards the invaders but was stopped in his tracks by a soldier using a night vision rifle equipped with a silencer. Michael knew that the sudden cessation of the barking meant his pet had met his Maker and he wasted no time in activating a prearranged alarm call to his team.

The commander outside his house contacted HQ, "We have a problem, the suspect's dog has alarmed the suspect and I request we bring the attack forward immediately!"

"Request agreed. All systems go! Repeat all system go!" came the immediate reply.

The troops battered the target properties from all sides, causing complete chaos within the various households. The occupants of the properties were mesmerized when faced with the black balaclava SAS troopers carrying submachine guns forcing all members of the families to lie on the floor.

Not everything had gone to plan as the invading forces had missed two of the targets. Mhairi McClure was in London, carrying out her own military exercise and Pat Kearney, who had left his house late the previous evening to go on an all-night fishing trip. O.L.S. was considered a success and all the other ringleaders of The 1972 Club were flown to the British mainland for questioning by MI5.

Mhairi had returned to her hotel before she picked up the warning signal from Michael and immediately using Gavin's phone put a call through to a nunnery in Norfolk where her school friend Gwen O'Connor was ensconced. "Gwen, Mhairi here, I've got a problem which I can't discuss over the phone. I need your help, can I come up to Norfolk?"

"Yes, of course Mhairi. The Lord is used to looking after waifs and strays." laughed the Mother superior, "See you soon."

Chapter 42

Michael Caldwell was shown into a very bare grey interrogation room and told to sit at the metal table in the middle of the room which was surrounded by six blue cushioned chairs. Two soldiers stood on guard.

Twenty minutes later the door opened and Brigadier Tate accompanied by AB and his personal assistant entered the room. "Morning Chancellor Caldwell, I'm Brigadier Tate, this is Armitage Brown and his colleague Carlton Montague." There were no handshakes as the Brigadier continued "you may remember me from when I was serving in Northern Ireland twenty odd years ago when, I recall you were at Queens University and were someone we could rely on. I can't express how surprised I was to find someone of note caught up in this threat to citizens in Scotland."

Michael shrugged his shoulders and looked the brigadier in the eye, "Times, but also people change Brigadier and,

237

if my son had not been killed in the crossfire created by your troops I probably wouldn't be sitting here."

An embarrassing flush came over Tate's face before he spoke quietly, "I'm sorry, I was completely unaware of your loss. Unfortunately, war situations throw up actions that punish the innocent."

AB took a harder line realising that the brigadier had been caught off his guard.

"Mr Caldwell you're here because your plot to extract £20m from her Majesty' coffers has been exposed and you, along with the other leading traitors of the 1972 Club have been rounded up and brought over to the mainland for interrogation. As we speak they are being questioned by members of my staff."

"Who are 'they', if I might ask? "enquired Caldwell.

"Let me see" replied AB picking up a sheet of A4 in front of him, 'David Cossar, Seamus Carr, Colm Murphy, Mhairi McClure and Pat Kearney. As a result of house raids we carried out they're all here." AB lied. "You are all facing long prison sentences as your proposed crime involved threatening Customs & Excise. I don't have to tell you that they have far greater powers than the police and do not take lightly to being threatened. However, if you cooperate with us I promise you it will be in your interest and may reduce the time you spend at her Majesty's pleasure. Our enquiries are still at an early stage but already the charges include assassination, murder, money laundering and extortion so I think you better come up with some pretty good answers tout suite."

Michael Caldwell took a sip of water before making his statement. "The plot was my idea, Colm and Mhairi were party to it, but have not to date made any contribution to its success. Seamus Carr did assist us in enlisting the help of John Gourley who planted the explosives in casks at the Scotia Distillery. Gourley was told that if he went to the police or leaked information to anyone he would be killed. Unfortunately, as you know he died as a result of a freak accident in Rome."

"David Cossar used his contacts to acquire the six Semtex explosives which we planted in whisky casks over a period of months. These are now currently lying in whisky bonds awaiting detonation which would most likely bring devastation to the surrounding communities. Only Pat Kearney and I know the specific numbers of the barrels containing the Semtex and where the remote controls are to activate them. I am also holding a strong bargaining tool gentlemen and hesitancy on your part could result in some early Millennium fireworks!"

"Hold on a minute Caldwell. You're not seriously trying to blackmail us into letting you and the others walk away from a very serious crime." protested the Brigadier before continuing, "You say that only Pat Kearney and yourself have fingers on the button but you don't strike me as someone who would carry out such carnage. Kearney, on the other hand is a nasty bastard and most likely to be the one who has access to the explosives. Unfortunately, he has to date escaped custody."

Michael smiled, "PK has escaped custody? You said earlier he was in here somewhere. Well that's good to know, so now you do have a problem."

AB exhaled a sigh of resignation, "Okay, that's enough. Mr Caldwell, please can you leave the room while I speak with the Brigadier."

"Certainly, Mr Brown. I look forward to seeing you again shortly." At that he left in the company of the two military police in the room.

As soon as the door closed AB launched into a scathing attack on Brigadier Tate, "What the hell are you doing Brigadier giving Caldwell information about Pat Kearney? He had no idea about whom we have arrested so we were more likely to get information if we adopt a 'divide and rule' policy. Please in future be mindful about what you say!"

Brigadier Tate held up his hands in apology, "Sorry Armitage, I got caught up in the moment, it won't happen again."

"Okay, understood. Carlton bring Mr Caldwell back for further interrogation."

Michael re-entered the interrogation suite and facing his foes started off the conversation with, "Well gentlemen, I trust you have resolved your unfortunate leak and we can now discuss how best to rectify the current situation to the satisfaction of all concerned."

"You impudent bastard!" bellowed AB, "You don't have a negotiating position and, if I have my way you'll be locked away for the rest of your life along with your collaborators."

"Mr Brown" answered the academic, "you're forgetting something PK, Pat Kearney to you, is out there somewhere on the loose with the ability to detonate at will five barrels of whisky that will act as a catalyst to cause huge explosions and wreck carnage all over Scotland. Possibly resulting in possible mass casualties. Once PK realises that the rest of The 1972 Club committee have been rounded up he, and probably some of his henchmen, will head for Scotland. Only he and I know the exact whereabouts of the explosive devices some of which are in high density areas, so time is not on your side. I am prepared to give you the vital information regarding where to find the explosive devices provided we can all walk free. You can then get your bomb disposal service to neuter the explosives and everyone will be happy."

"That's preposterous, the Government will never agree to that." snarled the Brigadier.

Michael Caldwell retorted with a logical response.

"Why not? Our demands have not reached the media yet apart from Hugh Ramsay at the Caledonian in Edinburgh. I'm sure you can buy his silence easily enough. If PK bombs the targets and it comes out that MI5 and the military failed to prevent the disaster then you guys will go down in history as the men who failed the nation. At this point I will need a lawyer so that we can draw up a formal agreement that he can present to the press if you fail to fulfil my conditions.

"Give us details of your legal advisors and I'll have them here in a few hours." signalled AB.

"My man is Paul Lynch of Connelly & Co in Coleraine."

AB turned to Carlton Montague, "Phone Lynch immediately and let him speak to Mr. Caldwell. Explain we require his presence and are providing air transport to get him here as soon as possible. Once he arrives Mr Caldwell we shall reconvene."

Paul Lynch was having a family day at his house in Coleraine when he got the call from Michael Caldwell which left him completely mystified. He immediately packed a bag and waited for a car to take him to a RAF base for the journey to MI5 headquarters in Whitehall. He made a detour to his office to pick up a folder giving him details of all Michael Caldwell's affairs.

By eight o'clock Paul Lynch arrived at MI5 and, before sitting down with the British Government representatives to re-commence negotiations, he requested some time with his client, which was granted.

"Michael what's going on"' asked the slightly-built balding figure peering over his rimless spectacles.

"Paul, thanks for coming. Let me explain the situation." The Chancellor then described everything to his brief.

By the time he finished talking Paul Lynch was speechless, "Michael this is unbelievable and very, very serious. You and your colleagues might never see the light of day again if these charges are proved correct."

"I'm aware of that and that is why I have put some doubt in their minds after they let it slip that Pat Kearney had escaped their clutches. They can't afford not to seek a compromise so I intend giving them the details of where they can find the explosives in the whisky casks but only once you and their legal advisors had drafted an amnesty for the individuals they are holding. We have to act quickly as I am concerned that PK will activate the

Semtex and kill hundreds, if not thousands of people. That is something I don't want on my conscience."

"Well here's hoping it doesn't come to that Michael."

The atmosphere in the interrogation room changed when the discussions continued. The MI5 team had been increased to include two legal experts and both parties were far more co-operative - especially after Michael Caldwell told him of his fears for PK's actions. Looking across the table Michael Caldwell cleared his throat before asking, "Gentlemen do we have a deal?"

AB's face tightened as he clasped his hands firmly then replied drily. "Yes. I have spoken to the Home Secretary and she has agreed to a pardon - provided no harm comes to any British citizens as a result of your actions. Let's get on with it, Mr. Caldwell. Where are the explosives?"

Paul Lynch took a letter out of the folder in front of him and passed it to Michael.

Opening the letter Michael spoke, "The explosives were placed in whisky casks over a three-month period at the Scotia Distillery in Edinburgh by John Gourley before they were consigned to be bonded at different warehouses throughout Scotland, where they could do maximum damage. This letter, of which I have copies, lists the details of the filling dates, casks numbers and storage details.'

The paper was passed across the desk to Armitage Brown and Brigadier Tate who huddled together to examine its details. The Brigadier gave out a disgusted reaction, "God you people really are evil. I can't even start to think how the emergency services would have coped with this lot if it all went up at the same time and what the casualty rate would have been!"

AB reaction was more constructive, "My sentiments exactly, Brigadier. Our immediate job now is to put an end to this threat. Can you please scramble the bomb squad immediately and get them to make Scotland a safer place in which to live? Get on to the Air Force as well, we will need helicopters to transport them on site as soon as possible."

The bomb squad headquarters at Craigiehall, just outside Edinburgh was on high alert and put into practice procedures which they had rehearsed many times. It was not long before they were arriving at their five target destinations to carry out controlled explosives on the suspect whisky casks.

Chapter 43

PK looked at the four 'soldiers' he had assembled round the table before supplying them with their brief. They were all proven killers, fanatical to the United Ireland cause and to whom he would trust with his own life. Before the meeting he had taken it upon himself not to mention the £20m. ransom for fear of being asked some embarrassing questions as to who would be the major beneficiaries of the proceeds.

"Morning men, 1972 platoon has a major problem. Everyone on our committee has had their properties raided last night. They were arrested and taken by the British to some as yet unknown secret destination. The reason for this is that we were planning to hurt the British economically by blowing up large portions of the whisky stocks but somehow their intelligence services have got wind of it. However, that doesn't mean to say that's the end of it. I have a list of where the bombs are planted and Michael Caldwell left the remote-control devices with me so the programme can go ahead. I should emphasise that we do not want this to result in huge loss of lives so warnings will be given to allow the emergency services to clear the areas near the whisky bonds."

"That's very clever PK so it is. When do you plan to carry this out?" Jake Brady enquired.

PK looked closely at the group before replying, "I have already made arrangements for us all to go in a fishing boat tonight which will leave from Port Stewart and will drop us off somewhere on the Ayrshire coast not too far from one of the targets in Girvan. Liam Henderson will take care of this target. Jake, you can get a bus into Glasgow Buchanan Street Bus Station then switch to another bus for Shettleston, another target area. Peter Wilson and Frank Gilhooley will get a car supplied by our colleagues, sympathetic followers of our cause, who are based in the West of Scotland. The car will be left at the Ardrossan Ferry Terminal and from there you can drive over to Clackmannanshire. Here, there are two of the biggest whisky bonds in the country at Alva and Hillfoots so plan your attack wisely. After the warnings are given there will be congestion, so make sure you are near enough before you press the detonators. That only leaves me. I am heading for Leven on the Fife coast by train from Glasgow, changing in Edinburgh, then arriving at Markinch, which used to be a whisky town before all the production was moved to Lundin Bonds. It now hosts huge whisky stocks in the bonds ready for bottling later which is the majority of blended whisky produced anywhere. From Markinch I will get into Leven and do the necessary there."

"Any questions?"

"No. Ok then we will meet here at 5 o'clock this afternoon. Only limited luggage and no guns. They will also be made available when we arrive in Scotland." Chapter 44

Mhairi arrived back at the Lancaster Hotel in time for breakfast which she skipped after reading the text from Michael. Quickly changing into casual gear, she left her room and the hotel without saying goodbye to Gavin O'Reilly and lost herself in the London traffic. She stopped along the way to buy a new phone before throwing the old one into the River Thames. Mhairi had prepared herself for this day which she hoped would never come. Carrying both credit and debit cards issued under the name 'Francoise Lyon' by the Bank of Luxembourg, she purchased train tickets to Norfolk without attracting the attention of the local constabulary.

When she didn't appear for breakfast Gavin O'Reilly went into the adjoining room in his suite to see if she was alright, after the early Sunday morning traumas but there was no sign of her. Thinking Mhairi had stepped out to buy something Gavin didn't panic, but after a couple of hours passed, he was getting a bit tetchy.' What if she had suffered a reaction after the killing of Colonel Inglis and had gone to the police?' he asked himself. He summoned his bodyguards together and instructed them to sanitize the Irishwoman's room as best they could, packing all her luggage into a suitcase which they would take back to the United States on his private jet. If Mhairi made contact he would return her worldly goods. He considered that his plan was better than leaving them for the police to mull over. The O'Reilly party then headed for Gatwick and would be back in the Boston before the news of Colin Inglis's death was exposed in the Monday morning headlines of the newspapers.

The confession box was uniform, dark with a grill to communicate with the priest on the other side. The priest cleared his throat, then asked Mhairi how he could assist her. Mhairi looked into the grill before beginning, "Forgive me father for I have sinned - more than once." "And in what way my daughter?

"Father, yesterday I assisted in the assassination of a Colonel Colin Inglis, the man who killed my fiancée in 1982, and before that I was an accessory in the murder of David Johnston in Belfast in 1988."

"This is extremely serious and very much a police matter. How do think the Holy Father should forgive you?"

"I feel my life is at an end and I cannot face being locked up. I would ask that I be allowed to take Holy Orders and serve the church in the way I almost did after my fiancée Matt O'Reilly was shot. I would be giving up the materialistic life I have been leading and would arrange the transfer of my assets totalling millions of pounds, currently held in overseas tax havens, to be given over to the Vatican."

A pregnant silence was followed by a short, sharp, response from the priest. "There is no way the Church can offer you absolution at the present time. Come back here again in two days." At that point, the confession window closed and Mhairi burst into tears and fled from the box, into the comforting arms of Gwen O'Connor and the sanctuary of the convent.

The priest did not waste time in getting back to Mhairi under the camouflage of the confession box. "Mhairi, since we last spoke I have consulted the Holy See in Rome and they are concerned about the level of your crimes but are prepared to take a compassionate view on the basis that one of your victims ruined your life. Your crimes prevent you taking Holy Orders but we will allow you to go to Rome under a new identity of Sister Mary Kennedy, on a passport provided by Southern Ireland. Once there you will be seconded to the Vatican Bank, controlled by the controversial Cardinal Markeso, to serve your penance for the rest of your life and you will never again be permitted to leave the Vatican." And to date, she never has.

Chapter 45

The MV Adventurer interrupted its fishing and dropped anchor two miles off the Ayrshire coast. Twenty minutes later a motor launch came alongside and the five terrorists were transferred on board and transported to the marina at Wemyss Bay before they dispersed to carry out their deadly missions.

Martin Bird the editor of the Fife Free Journal was interrupted by Jim Greer, his crime reporter, who copying the caller's Irish accent announced that he had, quote, "The IRA on the phone".

Martin picked up the phone and listened as PK instructed him. "Mr Bird I need your assistance. Tomorrow my team will commence blowing up whisky bonds in different parts of Scotland in response to the British Government refusal to meet our demand for a £20m ransom fee. This is an economic attack on the British Government and I need your assistance to organize that these sights are cleared of all inhabitants as we have no desire to kill anyone. Talk to your equivalent in Edinburgh at the 'Caledonian' Mr Hugh Ramsay, and he will confirm where the whisky bonds in question are situated."

At that point, the phone went dead and Martin contacted Hugh Ramsay and relayed the warning message. Ramsay was a little miffed that the Irish had contacted a less prestigious newspaper. Wanting to hold on the exclusivity rights he had been promised by AB, he told Bird not to discuss his conversations with anyone and that he would have to sign the Official Secrets Act. Ramsay then phoned AB in Whitehall who welcomed the news that the terrorists were planning to be in Scotland where his surveillance teams would be in position to apprehend them. The bomb squads were already on their way into the threatened whisky bonds and he had little doubt they would call back to him to confirm they had made all the explosive devices safe.

Captain Paton was co-ordinating his bomb disposal teams from his office in Craigiehall. He was pleased when the teams at Shettleston, Girvan, Alva and Hillfoots all confirmed that they had located the terrorist threat and carried out controlled explosions. He waited anxiously for Lieutenant Mike Spalding to complete the sequence before reporting back to MI5 but after an hour he had not received any news. So, he made a call to his man at Lundin Bond.

"Mike, Captain Paton here, how's it going? All the rest of the team have carried out successful operations and it is not like you to be lagging behind."

"Morning sir, we have a problem here, I have carried out tests on cask no.13212 but there is no explosive device to be found anywhere."

"Shit no!" interrupted Spalding's commander. "Have you checked any other casks.'

Yes Captain. Dave Young the warehouse manager is in the process of breaking out the batch of two hundred casks that were delivered to Lundin on 16th March for James Stalker Distilleries. This will take time and I'll get back to you as soon as I have any results."

"Okay Mike I will have some of the boys helicoptered in to Leven to help your team. MI5 have just told us that the terrorists who are going to ignite the attack are now in the area. We have to find this device, all the rest of them have been removed by controlled explosion."
"Oh God, Sir that's bad news. Talk to you soon."

AB was relaxing in his office for the first time for a while when his door burst open, without a knock, and Carlton Montague blurted out, "AB we have a problem. Bomb disposal have just reported that they are unable to detect the device in cask No. 13212 at Lundin Bond."

AB's face went white as a sheet as his mind scrambled about what to do next. Speaking out loud he analysed the situation.

"The terrorists have said they will attack sometime in the next twenty-four hours but asked for all civilians to be cleared from the danger areas. This had not been done due to the other bombs being neutered and the traps set in the hope of arresting the guilty parties. It would be a major logistical exercise for the emergency services to do it now in the time given. When the attackers see that their instructions have not been adhered to they will communicate amongst themselves and may call the action off. However, if one terrorist based at a location

"

where the bomb disposal has made it safe detonates a device that fails, then they will know they have been exposed. If all five bombs are detonated simultaneously at a given time then a large part of Leven will disappear off the map!"

"Carlton get Michael Caldwell in here now!"

Prisoner 1561895 aka Michael Caldwell arrived within minutes to face a stern looking Armitage Brown and his support staff. AB wasted no time in wading into the Chancellor.

"Caldwell what game are you playing? We sent the bomb squads to diffuse the explosives planted by your gang and four teams reported back with a positive outcome. The fifth suspect cask" he said shuffling the papers on his desk, "eh, at Lundin Bond in Leven is not there. The officer in charge of the bomb disposal has checked all the other whisky barrels which were sent there that day and has come up with a complete blank."

Michael responded, "I... I... don't understand how it is not there? That was the cask number I received from John Gourley."

"Are you sure man, think, there could be hundreds of lives at stake. Your killers made a call to a local newspaper to say that they were in Scotland to carry out your wicked plan, which we have managed to thwart with the exception of Lundin Bond."

 Lundin Bond!" cried out Caldwell "that's where Pat Kearney was heading! He wanted to be where not only the bonds, but also the production unit, would be destroyed causing the maximum amount of damage to your Exchequer."

"Christ, it gets worse" spluttered Brigadier Tait, "That madman is very likely to carry out his task without giving any consideration to loss of life and may even go down with it to seek martyr status in IRA history books. Caldwell are you positive that 13212 was the correct number you were given by Gourley?"

"YES, I AM, BUT THE ONLY MAN WHO CAN CONFIRM IT IS DEAD!!"

Seizing his opportunity, AB retaliated in a loud voice, "Well Mr Caldwell you have failed to supply us with accurate information and therefore in terms of the Amnesty agreement the Home Office sanctioned previously - ALL BETS ARE NOW OFF!!"

Shock filled the Irish academic's face as he contemplated the future for his colleagues and himself.

Carlton Montague broke the prevailing silence, "Gentlemen, can I suggest we go back to the source of our problem and get in touch with Scotia Distillery."

"Ok, do that Carlton", directed a now rather dour, angry Armitage Brown, "But I'm not hopeful they can help. In the meantime, Brigadier Tate alert the Emergency Services and see how we can minimise the risks."
Chapter 46

253

"

Jack Cockburn's wife answered the phone to a polite English male accent who asked, "Mrs Cockburn, is Jack there?"

"Yes, I'll get him." she replied, "Jack it's for you."

"Hello Jack Cockburn."

"Jack, Derek Phillips here. We have a bit of a problem regarding the Spirit Store which needs to be sorted out tonight. I have sent a car for you which should be with you in ten minutes. Come right into the Customs Office when you arrive, where I will be waiting for you." The phone clicked dead.

Jack felt his bowels move with the thought that Phillips had uncovered his ploy of smuggling white spirit out the distillery in a plastic bag stitched into his raincoat. If caught he would lose not only his job and pension rights but would end up in jail. True to Phillips word the car arrived to take him the short journey to the distillery. Jack's heart sank further when he saw it was a police car which set off with its blue lights flashing as soon as he fastened his safety belt.

Derek Phillips the Customs Surveyor who had more power than most police chiefs were looking over the ledgers that contained all the filling details for 16th March 1999 when Jack entered his office.

 Jack, sorry to drag you out but we have high security risk which involves your work in the spirit store." Jack felt his legs buckle but managed a reply.

"How does it involve me?"

"Someone has put an explosive device in one of the casks filled on 16th March 1999 but so far bomb disposal has failed to locate it. It was supposed to be No.13212 but it is not in there. You and Willie were on duty that day but he is away on holiday so that leaves you to help us."

"Let me think", said a relieved Jack looking at the filling sheets,"16th March 1999 going to Lundin Bond. It is a long time ago and we send stock there nearly every day. If there was anything wrong with a cask, for instance if it was leaking, we put it aside and rack it but there's a record of all racked casks down in the store and also on the filling sheets." Turning the page Jack exclaimed "Ya beauty! There it is Mr Phillips, cask no R13336 was a racker which was held back from the day before as, if I recall correctly, we were in a hurry to get the CLV (Crown Locked Vehicle) away so that it could get to Leven before the bond closed for the night."

"Thanks Jack, I'll pass this information on to my colleagues at MI5 who will be elated." said Phillips turning into the cupboard and coming out with a bottle of Old Parr Scotch Whisky, "Here take this as a token of our gratitude."

A relieved Jack Cockburn stammered out, "Thanks very much Mr Phillips."

AB received the good news and passed it on to Captain Paton Immediately. R13336 was found within minutes

"

and taken from the warehouse to a safe site where Mike Spalding and his team confirmed that it contained an explosive device. Mike phoned Captain Paton for further instructions, "Sir we have the rogue cask and can confirm that it contains an explosive device. Do I have permission to carry out a controlled explosion?"

Captain Paton thought about it for a moment before answering, "Remove the danger to a secure place but do not destroy the evidence at this stage." Paton kept the phone in his hand while dialled a call to MI5. "Mr Brown, we have found the missing hogshead and my men have removed it to a safe place well away from the whisky bonds. Do you want it destroyed immediately or would you prefer that we leave it and let Pat Kearney detonate what effectively will be a controlled explosion which will not endangering the public? Using GPS, we can locate him in seconds."

"What a brilliant idea Captain! I would like to catch Pat Kearney then we could put the whole gang away for a very long time, with the exception of the McClure woman with whom we will catch up with later. How can we clear the town in time to make the IRA think that we are still looking for their planted bombs?"

 I would suggest that we put out a media release stating, 'A small WW2 bomb has been discovered In Leven therefore the road will be closed to through traffic.' This will bring everything to a halt."

AB took control, "Okay leave this to me. I'll get all the emergency services and media companies involved and by tomorrow morning the area around Leven will be cleared. How large do you want the no- go area to be?"

Paton paused for a second, "To make it authentic I would make it one and a half miles either way. We have the advantage of knowing there will be a controlled explosion taking place which will justify our decision, in the general public's eye, for clearing the area."

All the plans were put into place. Residents were moved to church halls and given overnight accommodation; petrol stations advised to close down their petrol pumps and the workforce at Lundin Bond told not to come in to work the next day. The latter was not well received by the local management. Armitage Brown spoke to the Chairman of the whisky conglomerate at his London headquarters and explained how MI5 had stopped a major attack on the Scotch whisky industry and that alleviated any local difficulty.

Although AB and his team had worked all through the night, they still convened a meeting at 9.00a.m. in MI5 headquarters to verify that everyone knew their role in O.L.S. Earlier that morning AB accompanied by Brigadier Tate and Carlton Montague met with a very dishevelled and worried looking Michael Caldwell who now realised that the possibility of his plans becoming a reality was growing increasingly stronger by the minute.

"Morning Mr Caldwell, your friend Pat Kearney has been in touch with the local Fife press to say that his team will be in position today to launch their attack. As we explained yesterday with your co-operation we were

"

able to locate four of the stricken whisky hogsheads but so far unfortunately not the one at Lundin Bond so...."

"No", screamed the academic, "You have to find it. PK knows that you are holding us so the game is up for him and he will blow the fucking place to smithereens!!"

Just the reaction I was hoping for thought AB before continuing, "We have been working through the night clearing the Leven area moving the local population to safety but what we don't know is when this attack is likely to take place. Do you Chancellor Caldwell?"

Michael Caldwell had slumped forward, placing his elbows on the table and his head between his hands. As his body shook uncontrollably he began sobbing openly. Looking up, with tears running down his cheeks he nodded, before clearing his throat. "One of the things PK and I have in common is we both like old cowboy films, so we decided upon the Gary Cooper classic 'High Noon.'

"Thank you, Mr Caldwell, I'll inform the local area commander. We have set up CCTV cameras around the Lundin complex so we will be able to watch what happens to the site should the bomb not be found by then. Your attendance is essential to witness the mayhem you have managed to create." The crumpled heap, that was once a confident educationalist, did not manage to muster a recognisable reply.

Chapter 47

PK had arrived in Leven early and hid himself in the attic of one of the abandoned houses high up near the woods above the town, about eight hundred yards from the whisky bonds He had told his team only to contact him by text so was surprised when a call came in. "PK, Jake here, the boys are all in position but the authorities have not cleared the target areas and there is a huge chance that there will be a considerable loss of life if we carry on."

PK retorted, "That is not what's happening here where they have cleared the streets and sent the workforce home. I can understand your predicament so I will leave it up to your conscience as to what you do at twelve o'clock but I am going to carry out as planned."

He closed the phone off and made his way up into the woods through a series of back gardens and used all his army skills to conceal himself for the planned assault.

The MI5 Conference Hall in Whitehall was busy with a cross section of the great and the good including the Chiefs of Staff for all three Armed Service, Emergency Service Heads Cabinet Ministers and the top brass from MI5. Even the Chairman of the Scotch Whisky Association occupied a ringside seat. At 11.45 Michael Caldwell was shown into the room wearing a checked twill shirt, brown cords and a Harris Tweed sports jacket. Armitage Brown signalled that his men bring him to the front row, "Sergeant, handcuff this man to the chair, Caldwell, if we are to suffer watching the consequences of your devastation then so will you!" Michael was thrust unceremoniously into the chair just as a message came over the sound system.

"Mr Brown, Captain Paton here, we have carried out our final sweep of the bonds but have still not found the missing bomb."

A dark murmur filled the room at the disappointing news before AB replied in a very sombre tone, "That is bad news, so it looks like the terrorists have won on this occasion."

"I'm afraid so," Commented Captain Paton.

Everyone sat gazing at the large screen with the clock in the left-hand corner making its way to midday. Many of attendees looked at Michael Caldwell with anger in their eyes at what he was about to carry out in the name of republicanism.

They were not the only ones looking at the clock, Pat Kearney was battling with his conscience. "If I abandon this, all our planning will be for nothing. If I carry on, the Irish Movement will benefit from all the publicity the attack will receive and The 1972 Club will have shown the official IRA they disagree with The Good Friday Agreement."

His digital watch turned to midday and he pressed the detonator.

The clock on the large screen in Whitehall approached 12.00 and Michael Caldwell closed his eyes tight before two seconds later the sound of the huge explosion filled the room at which point the Irishman's bowels gave way. Everyone was looking at the screen for further structural damage but none was forthcoming.

AB stood up and addressed the assembled company, "Gentlemen what you have just witnessed was a controlled explosion carried out by the bomb squad, The Home Office took a decision not to inform you prior to our gathering for security reasons. I am pleased to announce that our surveillance teams at the various targeted whisky bonds have been successful in arresting a number of terrorists at sites in Girvan, Glasgow and Clackmannanshire."

"However, the action is not all over for today, as the police and MI5 hope to confront the remaining unaccounted-for terrorist, Pat Kearney, who is still at large." Turning to his side he continued, "Soldier, could you please remove the odorous Mr. Caldwell and return him to his cell."

The sound of the bomb going off was music to PK's ears but the silence that followed was puzzling and unwelcome. What had gone wrong? He remained in his position for a few minutes. A klaxon went off sounding the all-clear and the inhabitants of Leven plus all traffic started to move almost immediately.

Down in the town Superintendent Harper was standing next to Captain Paton when the Semtex went off, "Good we have a signal. Our man is in the woods up there", he said pointing to the trees above them. Harper looked at the map of where he had stationed his force.

Picking up the telephone connecting him to his team of armed officers he began, "Sections 41 and 42 the suspect is in your area. Approach him with caution as he is probably armed. Back-up is on the way."

Coming out of the woods PK looked in both directions. To his left there were a couple of armed response officers about six hundred yards away, who made him back into the trees again out of their view. To his right were a young couple in their late twenties dressed in jeans, trainers, and parkas, both wearing woollen hats. They were pushing a buggy which had seen better days. As they approached, arguing ferociously amongst themselves in the local Fife dialect, a child bawled loudly from the pram.

PK took in the scene. "Perfect", he thought, "just the hostages I need to act as my passport out of here", as he felt for the automatic pistol tucked under his coat.

The couple were now about twenty feet away and the confrontation continued, "Jenny, I tell't you, I didnae want this brat in the first place. All it does is shit and cry frae morning to night!' the man shouted before continuing, "I've had enough. He's doing my heid in, I'm going to finish this once and for a'."

At that he pushed Jenny to the side and taking the buggy with two hands he swung it like a hammer thrower, through the air, down the embankment as infant sounds continued to fill the air.

Horror filled PK's Face, watching as the pram travelled in what seemed like slow motion as it landed down the embankment before turning over several times. PK had never seen anything like this in his life.

"What the Fu..!! "he cried, moving to within six feet of the young couple, but before he could complete his obscenity, they both produced Taser guns from their jacket pockets. They fired an electrical charge into his body rendering him paralysed.

The woman quickly moved towards the injured terrorist removing all weaponry from PK's twitching body while her colleague fastened on handcuffs. A dazed Pat Kearney managed to utter, "What about the bairn?"

The woman replied in an accent entirely different from before, "There was no baby in the pram only a doll that made a lot of noise. Our intelligence was correct, when they said you had a soft spot for young children."

The male officer made a phone call to Superintendent Harper, "Section 42 here Sir, we have apprehended the suspect successfully, we require back-up and an ambulance to transport him to Area Headquarters." Other officers arrived along with an ambulance which drove Pat Kearney to Kirkcaldy to be officially charged and then, after his full recovery to Edinburgh Airport, on the first part of his journey to Whitehall.

Back at Whitehall, AB was able to announce Pat Kearney's capture to the assembled audience which was received with great applause. News was further transmitted out to all sections involved in 'O.L.S.' and it was greeted with jubilation throughout all the emergency services' stations in Scotland.

Angus Forbes, the Chairman of the Scotch Whisky Association (SWA) asked Armitage Brown if he could say a few words on behalf of his members.

He began, "Gentlemen the Scotch Whisky Association are grateful to all of your organisations for bringing today's proceedings to a successful conclusion. If events had turned out differently it would have set the Scotch Whisky industry back many years and it is doubtful if we could have retained our market position in view of new competition which would have flooded into the market during that period. Once again, thanks."

Chapter 48

"There you are Hughie. Six Castle Beers and two glasses to finish off the night on a beautiful February evening in the Cape. What could be lovelier than sitting here looking out over the Indian Ocean?"

Hughie McFaul had come out to South Africa for a holiday. The following day John and he had flown down to George then on to Wilderness where they had taken up residence at the Pink Lodge on the Beach, a large house which specialised in bed and breakfast. Earlier that evening, they had enjoyed a fabulous meal at 'Serendipity' the classiest restaurant in the area.

"This certainly is a beautiful spot John, I couldn't believe it when I went down on to the beach this morning and there was nobody to be seen for miles. Only dolphins making their way along the coast."

John responded, "The rooms are good and clean, so much so that I walked into the patio window. I wasn't badly injured but I told, Nellie, the owner, who said this often happens especially when the cleaner removes the warning stickers off the windows! One Scotsman she had here years ago hit it so hard he knocked out the window, frame and all. Fortunately, a disaster was prevented by the frame breaking its fall as it landed on a sunbed which duly shot off down the garden." Hughie laughed "A bit embarrassing."

"Yes, but the guest covered over his guilt by telling her a story about what happened to his wife, when she was recovering from hip replacement. They had met friends for coffee at the Royal Botanical Gardens in Edinburgh. His wife had booked a Motability scooter to get her round the hilly complex and off they went for coffee. One of the friends opened the door of the café and ushered her in. It was only at that point she realised she didn't know where the brakes were and ploughed straight into diners. One women saw her coming and held up her soup bowl in one hand and the spoon in the other as her table was shunted down the dining room!"

The pair chuckled into their beers at the thought of the scene before Hughie spoke in a more serious tone.

"John, just before the Millennium we made a number of arrests of Irish militants who had threatened the British mainland. They called themselves The 1972 Club and looking over their papers I think they were responsible for your dad's death."

The memory brought sadness to John and he surprised Hughie with his reply, "Yes that's right Hughie they were, Dad knew he was in danger. Just the day before he was killed he had stumbled upon a computer disc that was a complete dossier on the terrorist cell. He copied it and sent it to me inside a pair of football boots with a note that if anything happened to him we should hand it to the security services. Claude is friendly with someone at Mossad, the Israeli equivalent of MI5, so we passed it to them in return for my protection."

"Christ, you should have been in MI5. Not me!" exclaimed Hughie before continuing, "Remember my boss Colonel Inglis, whom you met at the rugby? Well, just about the same time as the arrests, he was assassinated in a park in London. Strange though, the bosses are not pulling out all the stops to find his killers."

"No Hughie, they won't. Your Colonel Inglis is the reason I came to South Africa. After one of our football matches when you went off in the huff because you couldn't get the ball off me, I witnessed a botched-up ambush involving Colonel Inglis." John then told Hughie everything that happened back in 1982.

"I couldn't believe it when you introduced us at Twickenham. I think you sensed something was wrong with me that day."

"John, how have you coped with carrying all this around with you for such a long time?"

"Hughie my life seems been destined to be involved in political conflicts. Eighteen years ago, I had to flee 'The Troubles' in Northern Ireland to make a new life for myself in South Africa. I will be eternally grateful to my parents for making that decision as I have benefitted enormously from it. However, there are big changes going on here in South Africa since Nelson Mandela was released from prison seven years ago.

I was glad to see the end of the Apartheid system but so far, there has been slow progress for the indigenous population to raise their living standards. To date the authorities have managed to keep the lid on full scale uprisings. Improvements in education are the key to making South Africa, one of the richest countries in terms of agriculture and mineral wealth, a success. This is one of the best places in the world to live and failure to raise basic living standards will mean, as our housekeeper Jane once put it to me, 'Apartheid has just changed colour.'

Thankfully, Hughie the Ulster chapter of my life is finished now. I've thought a lot about it over the years.

Strange to think my journey all started with a game of football." John sighed before brightening up, "Well, time for bed."

The two young men smiled at each other, "Night Norman - sweet dreams."

Hughie concurred, "Night George - sleep tight."

SLAINTE!

A Gaelic toast used by whisky drinkers to wish you, the reader,

Good Health!

Acknowledgements

It has been extremely satisfying writing my first novel at the age of seventy - one, but this could not have been achieved without the support of friends and family.

Using my imagination and putting my ideas down on paper I have found a lot easier than proof reading the finished article. I would give thanks to my sisterin-law Norma Jenns and close friend Cathy Grandison for their proof reading services, my niece

Sharon Convery who helped with some technical aspects of 'Operation Large Scotch' and especially my sister Alison Anderson. Alison's enthusiasm for bringing the project to publication has been overwhelming and I could not have done it without her.

I have always been interested in writing and have produced the occasional business article in the past. The nearest I came to working on a book was back in 1995. As the Centenary Captain of Duddingston Golf Club in Edinburgh I acted as a researcher for the late, great sports writer Norman Mair, when he wrote our club history entitled 'Pillars of the Temple'.

Observing Norman closely, I found it fascinating how he could add his personal style to all the characters and 'Paint the pictures' for the reader.

I would recommend writing to other senior citizens as a hobby as it offers escape from the repetitive life retirement can become, and keeps your brain active.

All the above could not have come to a satisfactory conclusion without my understanding wife Joyce. Her devotion to our two grand-children Olivia and Austin freed up time for me to complete my book.

Bill Flockhart

Edinburgh 2017

71459622R00161

Made in the USA
Middletown, DE
28 April 2018